The Curse of Cliffe House

Will Macmillan Jones

First edition 2016 by Red Kite Publishing Limited

www.redkitepublishing.net

Text Copyright 2015 by Will Macmillan Jones

A CIP catalogue record for this book is available from the British Library.

Find out more about the author on
www.willmacmillanjones.com

Cover art by Hazel Butler: www.thebookshinebandit.com

ISBN

978-1535253635

CONTENTS

Books by Will Macmillan Jones

Paranormal Mysteries

The Mister Jones Collection

The Showing   2014

Portrait of a Girl   2015

The House Next Door   2016

The Curse of Clyffe House 2016

Demon's Reach   2017

Childrens Books

Snort and Wobbles   2014

Return of The Goblins   2015

The Headless Horseman   2016

Fantastically Funny Fantasy:

The Banned Underground Collection

Too many to list!

See www.thebannedunderground.com

Prologue

Robert turned over in the antique bed and sighed as he heard the springs of the old mattress move under his weight. In that ethereal state between waking and dreaming he reflected that elderly beds in solitary ancient holiday cottages were a hazard to be accepted when on solo walking tours of the Welsh countryside: at least he was only here for the one night before shouldering his rucksack and moving on. Even the dubious delights of this place that both looked and felt as if it still belonged to the Middle Ages were better than sleeping outside. Especially, he thought, as the rain was beating intermittently against the small, single glazed window. He hoped the weather would be better by the morning.

Then Robert froze. The mattress springs groaned under the shifting weight of another body - yet he was here alone. He could feel the motion as the other person rolled over and sat up. Although he didn't dare to move, Robert opened his eyes. Bright moonlight filtered into the room through the ill-fitting curtains. The intruder stood up, leaving the bed, and Robert heard the bedroom door open.

At last he found the courage to roll over and sit up. Warily turning his head, he saw that the bedroom door was now wide open and he could hear footsteps in the corridor leading to the main entrance. With a sudden surge of unexpected bravery, he flung the bedclothes away without noticing that the duvet on the other side of the bed had lain undisturbed. He heard the sound of a handle turning and Robert ran around the end of the bed and looked out into the corridor. The moonlight shone through the open front door, and he could see that he was alone.

The front door slammed shut, the sound terrifyingly loud in the silent cottage. Robert walked cautiously to the door, and looked out. Across the field, he could see a single figure slowly walking away from him. The person was wearing an ankle length white nightgown and had long auburn hair reaching halfway down the back of the gown: she was clearly female, and his instincts were stirred by her figure. Transfixed, he watched her walk away from him. Robert was inexplicably saddened as, driven by the wind, clouds drifted across the moon and she vanished from his sight. He turned back into the cottage and pushed his feet into his walking boots without bothering to tie the laces. He grabbed his jacket and strode out of the house, across the field. The light of the full moon shone again as the clouds shifted and there she was - ahead of him on the track that returned to the Coastal Path.

Her hair was mysteriously unmoved by the wind that tugged at his unfastened jacket, but Robert didn't notice. He was completely confused; who was this woman, and how had she been in his bed? Why had she been in his bed? He wanted answers to these questions, so he picked up his pace and walked faster towards her. Yet without seeming to increase her speed, she remained always ahead of him.

"Hey! Hey! Wait!" he shouted. She didn't seem to hear, and Robert shouted again. "Who are you? What do you think you were doing?"

She reached the gate that opened onto the Coastal Path, just as the rain started falling again. Robert cursed as he hurried after her, occasionally slipping as the path became muddy under his feet. At the gate, he stopped to catch his breath, yet she continued walking at that same deceptive pace, southwards now along the cliff top. The earthen track showed an occasional footprint in the mud, footprints that slowly filled with dark rainwater and reflected the brilliant full moon. Robert wiped the rain from his face and licked the water from his lips. He tasted salt and realised that the water was not rainfall but sea spray, driven over the top of the cliffs from the waves that lashed against the rocks far below.

Half slipping now on the mud Robert ran after the woman. At last, at a turn in the path, she stopped. Panting with the effort, he hurried towards her. The woman walked on for maybe ten paces and then stopped again. At last, thought Robert, he could catch this strange person. The surface became more slippery and treacherous under his feet, so he slowed his speed and walked towards her with some caution.

"No good going over the cliff," he said aloud to himself and took care in placing his feet. The edge of the cliff was perilously close; indeed the woman was standing now on a dark grassy spur away from the path. Still she faced away from him, but now the wind tugged at her nightgown, revealing a full figure that stirred his blood. Her hair began to stir and fly in the wind. As Robert slowed his steps further and finally approached her, she spread her arms wide to the wind and tilted her head back to bathe her face in the light of the full moon.

"Right," demanded Robert a little breathlessly, as he reached her. "Who are you, and what the hell were you doing in my cottage, in my bed? In my *bed*, for god's sake?"

The woman lowered her arms and turned to face him. With a gasp, Robert saw that she had no lips, no eyes, and no face: just a white skull, gleaming in the moonlight. Skeleton hands reached out for him. With a stifled scream, he staggered backwards and lost his balance. His feet slipped on the wet grass and falling he slid over the edge of the cliff. For an instant his right hand scrabbled vainly for a grip on the grass, then with a cry, he was gone to the welcoming mouth of the raging waves that thundered on the jagged teeth of the rocks a hundred feet below the Coastal Path.

The clouds briefly obscured the full moon, and when they were gone the cliff top was empty and silent.

Chapter one

I was comfortably enjoying the daily newspaper - if enjoying is the right word, and drinking tea when my next-door neighbour knocked on my door and walked in. Well, perhaps 'burst in' would be a better phrase as she was clearly in a state of some excitement.

"Mister Jones!" she exclaimed. "I've got some fantastic news! Oh, and a favour to ask!"

I lowered my newspaper, as she threw herself onto my sofa, waving a sheet of paper in her hand. "Sheila?" I asked. "Whatever's happened?"

"It's brilliant, Mister Jones!"

"What is?"

"You remember that I've been writing a book?"

"Well, yes, I remember you telling me all about it some time ago."

"An agent wants to see it!" Sheila could hardly contain her excitement.

"Sheila, that's fantastic news. Well done!"

Sheila Balsam thrust the piece of paper at me, and I took it. A literary agent had read the first three chapters and liked it enough to ask for sight of the full manuscript. "That sounds a wonderful opportunity for you, Sheila. I'm really pleased."

"Great! So, you'll help me?"

"Well, of course, but I don't really see what I can do to help you."

"I need you to come on holiday with me for a week, Mister Jones."

I leant back in my chair and looked at her. "Sheila, I know we are neighbours, but, well…"

"Oh don't be silly. I don't mean like that."

I started to sigh in relief but then smothered it in case I caused offence. My next-door neighbour and I are friends, but she is twenty years younger than I am, rather more heavily built and our personalities can clash. I am a more measured person, and her wild flights of fancy and enthusiasm would be a trial if they were inflicted upon me for any length of time. "Then what exactly were you thinking of, Sheila?" I asked cautiously.

"The thing is this. I didn't quite tell the agent the truth."

"Sheila!"

"I told them I'd finished the book, and I haven't actually managed that bit yet."

I felt a little relieved. This did not seem to me to be the most heinous of crimes. "Can't you just tell them that? I mean, if they liked the first part, won't they wait a bit?"

"Oh no, they won't do that!" exclaimed Sheila. "I have to send the whole thing off by the end of the month. So, I've booked this holiday cottage near the coast. I'd like you to come with me for the week while I write the last part of the book."

"Why?" I asked her, a little confused. "Sheila, I know we are friendly, but a holiday?"

She looked a little embarrassed. "Mister Jones, this is a bit awkward. The thing is, I'm a bit scared to go away on my own, and there's actually no one else I know well enough to ask. It's got separate bedrooms of course, and I'd just like a bit of company when I'm not writing. I'll pay of course."

"It's not the money, Sheila," I replied. "Just that, well..."

"I'm not bothered about my reputation, Mister Jones," she laughed. "And I know that I'm safe with you! In fact, that's one of the attractions."

I was unsure quite how I felt about that, and I think she realised.

"Oh, I didn't mean it quite that way. I meant that you are so, well, such a gentleman that anyone would feel completely safe in your company. And although I want somewhere a bit secluded so I can concentrate, it looks a bit wild for a girl on her own, if you see what I mean."

I was a little mollified, but not enough to feel enthusiastic.

"I'm depending on you," she said and gave me a pleading look.

"What am I supposed to do when you are writing?" I asked her.

"Whatever you normally do when you aren't working!" she replied. "There's reading, walking, it's near that Welsh Coastal Path and it's amazingly beautiful!"

Finally, I felt a little tempted. "I have always wanted to do some walking on that coast," I ventured. "The Coastal Path is well known for its beautiful scenery."

I should have realised that to a forceful person like my neighbour that was too much of an opening. At once she pounced, assuming that she had convinced me entirely.

"Excellent!" Sheila jumped up from my sofa, and to my surprise kissed me on the cheek. "I've already booked the cottage, so ring your boss and tell him that you're taking the next week off. I know you haven't taken any holiday time at all this year."

"How do you know that?" I asked her, as she spun round and bounced towards the living room door.

"Because you told me last month!" she replied over her shoulder and was gone in a flurry.

I was left, with my cooling cup of tea and now disregarded newspaper, to ponder what ill fortune had brought this new disaster into my life. And more importantly, which books I would need to take with me to help me to survive the coming week.

I experienced little trouble in getting my employers to accept a short notice holiday request. Indeed, there was so little fuss made that I left their building with a sense of mild unease, and a vague hope that my gainful employment would still be waiting for me on my return! In truth, I was beginning to feel enthusiastic about this enforced break. Sheila and I, while having no romantic entanglement, were quite good friends and it was entirely true that I had not had a break away from my job for quite some time. The change would indeed do me good I decided and began the unaccustomed task of packing with a smile.

Clothes were not a problem: while Sheila was writing I planned to do some walking on the wild Welsh coastline, and so I mainly packed warm and weather resistant stuff. Anyone who has experienced the joys of the Welsh Coastal Path will know that rain can be the most dependable weather. Then I added some books. A copy of the collected ghost stories of M.R. James seemed like a good idea, and something a bit lighter was also thrown into the case. So it was that when Sheila knocked on my back door early on the Saturday morning, I was well prepared and ready.

"Haven't you finished your tea yet?" she asked cheerfully. "Look, the weather's bright and everything!"

"I'll just wash up," I replied.

"Oh leave that! It will wait, and I can't!"

Sheila's evident happiness and delight at the idea of going away to write for a week was irrepressible, and I couldn't help but smile at her. Reluctantly I rinsed my cup in the sink rather than wash it properly, and leant past her to push the back door shut. "Just turn the key in it, please, Sheila," I asked her. Sheila locked the door from the inside.

"You'd better not tell me you haven't packed!" She wagged a finger at me as if I were a naughty child, and I laughed.

"Of course I have. Come on, the case is in the hall." I opened the door from the kitchen to the hall, and Sheila bounced through it and stopped abruptly.

"Er, Mister Jones..."

"What's up?"

"That case. It's a bit big."

I looked at the case, which in truth didn't seem very large to me. "It's the only one I've got, I'm afraid. What's the problem?"

Sheila walked down the hall and opened my front door. She pointed dramatically to her car, which was parked on her drive. To see what she meant, I had to follow her to the doorway and peer around both Sheila and the doorframe. The roof was down on her small Peugeot.

"The weather's so nice I thought it would be fun to drive with the roof off," she told me. "But that means there isn't much space in the boot, and I rather think I might have filled most of it myself." She looked dubiously at the rather elderly case that I had inherited many years ago from a now long dead relative, and had never had reason to replace.

"Will mine go on the back seat?" I asked.

Sheila looked at my case. "There's not a lot of room, but it's the only option. Come on then!" Putting the matter of my case behind her, she walked briskly across the garden towards her car. "Come on," she called back over her shoulder. "Hurry up!"

With a secret smile, I lifted my case, which in truth was not too heavy, and left the house. Carefully I made sure that the front door was properly secured while Sheila stood beside her car and tapped her foot impatiently. "Come *on* Mister Jones!" she called again. She didn't relax until I had lifted my case into the small space behind the rear seats and climbed into the passenger seat of the small car.

"Right!" she said brightly, and after starting the engine drove briskly off her drive.

"Do I need to navigate?" I asked her, looking around for a map.

Sheila laughed at me. "Of course not!" She tapped a small plastic box on the top of the dashboard. "This is a SatNav; it will tell me how to get to the cottage. It isn't all that far, anyway!"

The face of the device lit up, and after a moment started telling Sheila that she had taken a wrong turn. She pouted, and carried on regardless. "It will soon enough recalibrate and sort itself out," she told me. I hadn't seen one of the devices in action before and watched it with interest.

"I can sort of see the point, but personally, I prefer a map," I told her. I took out my Ordnance Survey map of the area, and with some difficulty in the small car, managed to unfold it to show our destination.

"Why ever don't you drive?" she asked me. "Haven't you passed your test?"

"Oh yes, of course I have," I explained. "But the buses are regular in the city where we live, so I don't really need a car. It would sit on my drive all week and rust."

Sheila tossed her head and let her long hair get picked up by the wind, and be dropped again. "I couldn't do without mine. Just couldn't." The SatNav gave her some insistent orders, and she promptly turned onto the motorway and accelerated towards the Welsh coastline. Before too long, we had left first the motorway and then the fast roads behind, and Sheila was driving, a little too quickly for my taste, along roads that became increasingly narrow and twisted alarmingly through the rolling green countryside.

At last, the SatNav turned us away from the more commonly used roads and we plunged into a network of back lanes whose hedges were high enough to obscure our view of the countryside. Sheila drove more slowly, to my considerable relief, and then stopped abruptly as a turn in the lane and a wide field gate suddenly revealed a stunning view. Deep green fields, dotted with bright white sheep formed a patchwork across the land, cut off at the end as if by a razor; here Cardigan Bay, an astonishing blue vision, sparkled under the sunlight.

"Wow," breathed Sheila. "That's just amazing."

"It's a really lovely day," I agreed.

Sheila reluctantly drove away. "I hope the cottage has such a good view," she said. "The online write up said it was close to the Coastal Path. Did you bring your camera?"

"It's in my bag," I told her. I was a little reluctant to say that rather than a new digital camera, I was still using an old film based Yashica SLR and hoping that I had brought enough rolls of film with me to use if the weather was going to give us days like this.

As we drove on, the hedges became less well cared for and trees appeared embedded in their line. The leaves overhung the narrow lane and blocked much of the sunlight from penetrating. Sheila drove more slowly and finally the SatNav told her to take the next turning on the left as we had arrived at the destination. She stopped and surveyed the unmade lane dubiously. "Do you think I can get down there?" she asked me.

I looked at the rough track, the ragged hedge with dark

overhanging branches and then at the bright and freshly painted signboard pointing down the lane. "I'm sure that we'll be fine," I said with a confidence that I did not in fact feel. "The sign says 'Fferm Ffynnon' and 'Clyffe House'. Is that right?"

"Yes. The cottage is in the grounds of a farm, I believe." Cautiously, Sheila turned onto the track, and drove slowly away from the lane. Every time the car lurched, one of the springs made an alarming noise, and she winced. The track turned twice and seemed to go on for a very long time but eventually some farm buildings came into view. They did not look very well kept, and I was conscious of a vague sense of unease. The farmhouse itself was almost a ruin. The roof had fallen in, and several of the windows were entirely free of glass. The front door sagged open and the green paint covering it was peeling and cracked. Sheila and I looked at each other in dismay, and when she pulled into the yard beside the house, Sheila did not turn off the engine.

"We can't stay here!" she said.

I didn't reply. That the house was uninhabitable was obvious, and besides the entire place had a lonely, neglected and desolate feel that I disliked intensely. The barns were unpainted, their roofs patched badly with corrugated iron. Brambles grew in wild profusion, blocking some of the doors to the outbuildings. Several of the outbuilding windows had been covered with unpainted plywood boards. The afternoon breeze suddenly carried a chill, and I shivered. From the corner of my eye, I saw Sheila do the same.

Then a collie dog, barking at us loudly, appeared around the side of one of the outbuildings, followed by its owner. Dressed in dingy but clean overalls, with rather well-worn wellington boots plastered in dried mud, this was clearly the owner. The shotgun carried casually in his right hand had an air of menace - but his expression was cheerful and friendly. I tried not to stare at the awful pockmarks from some past illness that had ravaged his face.

"Miss Balsam, is it?" he called as he walked across the yard towards the car. "I'm Davis. Iuan Davis. You'll be looking for the cottage? Clyffe House?"

"Er yes," replied Sheila. She looked again at the ruined farmhouse, and Mr Davis let out a huge laugh.

"Well, it's not this old place, bless you!" Using his gun, he pointed further down the lane. "About a quarter of a mile further on, you want. On the left it is, and a sight more welcoming than this old place. I've opened it up this morning to give it some air, what with the day being as it is. There's a fire ready laid for you for the night if you want it and the cooker runs on electricity, so you'll be fine."

"Thank you," Sheila replied, her smile reappearing.

"Now if you want anything," continued Mr Davis, "we live at Bryn Gelli. That's the farmhouse, just across the fields there." He pointed again with the gun, and we looked at a much better-kept farm about a quarter of a mile away across the fields. "You need anything, just come and ask."

"What about a key?" asked Sheila.

"A key? Bless you, I can tell you come from the city! Round here there's no need for locks and such. No one will bother you here."

"Thank you!" I replied, reassured a lot by his cheerful demeanour, and by the collie, which now ignored us completely. "What's this place then?"

"Oh, this is just the old farm, Fferm Ffynnon. I bought it years ago for the land. Always meant to do the old house up and sell it off, but never got around to it somehow. Anyways, go and settle yourselves in at the cottage and I hope you have a good week!" Mr Davis whistled to his dog and walked away. After a few strides he turned back. "But if you goes off walking and exploring, best you keep clear of this old place. Not in the best of states, it isn't, could be dangerous. So if you don't mind, I'd rather you gave it a wide berth. Then I'll sleep more easily." He chuckled.

"Of course!" I agreed.

Mr Davis smiled cheerfully again and waited until Sheila reversed out of the decaying farmyard, and drove on slowly down the rough track. His smile vanished and with some effort, Mr Davis pulled at an old metal gate until it surrendered and swung round to block the entrance. Taking some bright orange baler twine from his pocket, he tied the gate to the rusting metal post. He nodded to himself and with his collie dog trotting obediently at his heels, he walked off towards his own farmhouse. I had watched the whole performance in the wing mirror of Sheila's car but thought nothing more about it.

Very quickly we reached the holiday cottage. This was a long, single story building that was freshly whitewashed. The yard in front of the cottage was swept, and bright with flowers planted in tubs along the face of the building. At the gate, another freshly painted sign proclaimed 'Clyffe House'. As Mr Davis had promised, the windows were open to let the warm air in, and

Sheila smiled happily.

"I can smell the sea!" she exclaimed.

"So you should!" I pointed to the far end of the cottage, and there ran a path that led straight towards the bay. "We can't be more than a few hundred yards from the Coastal Path! And that sits on top of the cliffs, just there, look. If we are lucky, we might get to see some of the dolphins and seals that live in Cardigan Bay."

"That would be lovely," agreed Sheila. Stopping the car near the open front door, she reached down and pressed a button on the console between the seats. With an unexpected whine that made me jump, the folding roof emerged from the boot and started to close.

The restoration of the building had been carried out really rather well. The front door opened directly into a narrow tiled corridor running the whole length of the building. In front of Sheila, without a door from the corridor, was a large living room with a varnished wooden floor. Deep windows in the far wall let in light, and the low ceiling featured thick wooden beams. A fire was laid in the fireplace, and old but comfortable looking furniture was placed around the room. Sheila flung her arms wide and spun round on the spot, to my considerable astonishment. I had followed her in through the front door with suitcases in each of my hands.

"Where are the bedrooms?" I asked.

"Isn't this just a lovely room?" she replied.

"Yes," I agreed. "Sheila, these cases are a bit heavy, where are the bedrooms?"

"Let's go and see," she answered and after pushing past me and the cases I carried, half ran back out of the living room into the corridor. She turned to her left away from the sea as I turned around with some difficulty. My case was indeed a little large for the room, which I saw as being rather cramped with furniture. Sheila's case bumped against the old sofa, and I muttered under my breath.

"Don't get grumpy, now!" called Sheila. She walked back across the front of the living room. "That way is the bathroom and the kitchen," she told me. "The bedrooms must be this way."

I followed her back into the hall. Two varnished oak doors were set into the wall, and a third was placed at the end of the hallway, facing down its length. I watched Sheila try the first two, which opened easily to her touch and let her glance inside. The third door didn't open.

"Can you try this one, Mister Jones?" she asked me. "It seems to be stuck!"

I put down the cases, and walked up to her, glancing through the open doors of the first two bedrooms as I went. I walked up to the third door and put my hand on the ancient, black-lacquered metalwork. The handle moved at once without fuss and the door opened.

"Huh!" she snorted and peered past me into the room. "Just like the other two inside, but it has a view towards the cliff. Would you mind if I took this one?"

Naturally, I did not. The choice seemed immaterial to me, and I turned back to get the case of hers that I had brought from the car. A muffled shout alerted me, and I looked at the bedroom door to see it was closed. I stepped close to the door and could hear Sheila shouting on the other side but couldn't make out her words as the antique door was such a tight fit that the sound was muffled. I opened the door, and Sheila was there frowning and a little flustered.

"The door closed, and again I couldn't open it!" she exclaimed.

I shrugged. "I don't seem to have a problem." I looked at the handle, and raised and lowered the latch again; it moved easily under my hand.

"Let me try," insisted Sheila. She grabbed at the latch mechanism, but again she couldn't make it move at all. "Perhaps you'd better have this one," she said thoughtfully. "No good my getting stuck inside, is it?"

I looked around the room. It seemed to be the same as the other bedrooms, with a double bed, an elderly Victorian wardrobe and a small chest of drawers. The only notable feature was a framed print that I vaguely recognised as a Millais painting called *The Somnambulist*.

"It's a nice room," I agreed. "Fine by me."

"Excellent," Sheila replied. Once more she tried the latch and gave up defeated by the immobile mechanism. "I'll go and make some tea; you bring in the rest of the cases?"

It wasn't quite a question, so I smiled and walked out of the room and down towards the front door. The door shut, and I could hear Sheila again try to open it and fail. "How odd," I muttered and then went off to bring our things in from the car.

Both the rest of the afternoon and the evening passed uneventfully. Sheila cooked some food, I washed up and then Sheila started to organise her notes for the rest of her book, planning to start her writing in the morning. I left her to her paperwork and took myself off to bed with a book. The bed was surprisingly comfortable, and before long I turned off the light and fell asleep. Later I awoke, and in that half awake, dreamlike state often felt in the middle of the night, I suddenly felt the mattress respond to the presence of another body sitting on the edge of the bed. The frame creaked and I was wide awake instantly. I felt the body stretch out fully on the bed, and I was unsure what to do. This was not how my relationship with Sheila was, nor indeed how I wanted it to be. I wondered how to approach the delicate issue of turning her away, turning her down.

Then I smelt an unfamiliar perfume and below that the overtone of the scent something else, something less pleasant. Something stale, or even rotting. I rolled over and sat upright. The bed felt strange, although I am unused to lying in a bed with another person: but still I could tell that something was not quite right. Sheila is, well to be polite, well built - yet the mattress did not feel to be occupied by a heavy person. I took a deep breath, and calling on a reserve of courage I did not know I possessed I opened my eyes, dreading what I might see. I had not closed the curtains and the moonlight streamed in through the deep window, shining across the bed and gleaming on the white calcified skeleton that lay beside me on the bed. The head turned to face me and I screamed in terror.

Chapter two

Sheila finished arranging the papers and notes she had brought and laid out on the low table in the living room. She looked over them, partly satisfied and partly concerned that there was not enough in the notes to help her finish the manuscript at the word count she had used in the submission to the agent. Something else was needed, she thought. The story was supposed to be frightening, but the element that should cause a reader to stay awake at night was missing, or not quite there yet.

She pondered the issue for some time without coming to a conclusion. Finally, she adopted the approach that has worked for many an author down the centuries: she decided to sleep on the problem. Obsessive about her personal hygiene she carefully brushed her teeth for over two minutes before changing into her red tartan pyjamas. Leaving the bathroom, she shivered slightly. The old house, a traditional Welsh longhouse, was still warm from the day but the varnished wooden floor felt cold under her bare feet.

"I should have brought my slippers!" she muttered to herself. Standing outside the door to the bathroom, she looked down the length of the hall. The rough stone wall to her left was still warm to the touch. The three windows let into the wall were dark: for although the moon had risen, the moonlight shone as yet on the other side of the house. A faint glow from the dying embers of the fire in the living room spread in a pool across the floor at the entrance to the living room and at the far end of the corridor the door to the bedroom Mister Jones had adopted was firmly closed. Sheila shivered unexpectedly as she thought about the strange catch on that door; how it had resisted all her attempts to open the door but had almost fallen open at the lightest touch from Mister Jones.

When she turned the bathroom light off, the hallway was dark. The faint fire glow was dying now. Sheila suddenly smiled. Maybe she could work the odd happening with the door handle into her book? "That would work!" she said aloud. The echo of her voice ran oddly down the corridor, for the house was very quiet. Even in the city suburb where she lived there was always some sound at night and Sheila felt vaguely ill at ease; the almost sepulchral silence was so unusual, not unexpected, but unsettling to a city dweller.

Walking towards her bedroom, Sheila stopped at the first window and looked out into the night. Although the yard in front of Clyffe House was in shadow, the moonlight lit the fields beyond the low, grey wall of local stone that marked the boundary of the holiday cottage. In the next field, a tall, solitary tree blocked a clear sight of the ruin of Fferm Ffynnon beyond. As she examined the view, the moon rose higher, and the cold light shone on the empty, glaring windows of the old house. The broken window frames seemed to leer at her like jagged, decaying teeth and Sheila shivered. In the darkness, with that eerie moonlight shifting with the thin clouds, the old house did not seem romantic at all. Rather it squatted behind the drystone walls and gave off a thinly veiled air of menace or threat. Sheila recalled Mr Davis' warning to stay away from the ruined farm, and thought that it was wise advice. She stepped away from the window and walked slowly down the corridor towards the room she had selected. At her bedroom door, she stopped. There was another window in the outside wall and again she looked out towards Fferm Ffynnon. This time, her view of the old house was not obscured by trees and the dilapidated state of the property was very clear. Beyond the far wall she could see the shadowed outbuildings, which were in better repair than the main house.

A hint of movement caught her eye as she was turning away and she again focussed on the old farmhouse. She was sure that she could see something white at one window, where before there had been only shadow. Yes! There it was. Was it, she wondered, a trick of the moonlight? The white image wavered and vanished. Curious, Sheila watched a little longer. The hint of bright white appeared then at the corner of the house and moved slowly towards the nearest outbuilding. It stopped by the door, and Sheila strained her eyes to watch. Clouds drifted across the moon, sending shadows racing across the whole scene and darkness fell over the old farm. When the cloud shadow left, Sheila could see nothing more to attract her interest. After a time she reached out, a little hesitantly, to the latch on the door to her bedroom. To her secret relief, the latch moved easily and the bedroom door swung open. Without a backward glance at the window, Sheila walked into her room and closed the door behind her.

"I'm just in the mood now to think of something really spooky to write," she said aloud. Sheila looked around the room, searching for something. There they were! Already on the bed, where she had placed them earlier. A large pad of A4 notepaper, and a sharp pencil. The essential tools for those authors who get their inspiration in the middle of the night and like to jot down their thoughts before the bright light of day dispels them. She turned back the thick duvet cover, switched

27

off the light and climbed into the bed, snuggling down into the warmth as the bedroom seemed to feel chill now; probably from the pale moonlight that filtered through the thin curtains.

Silence reigned over Clyffe House. Silence oozed from the darkly varnished roof beams that looked so quaint in the daylight. Silence stole through the single-glazed windows, and filtered down the chimney in the living room as the last embers of the fire flickered bravely and died. Silence rose from the sink in the kitchen, and dripped from the taps in the bathroom, flooding out under the closed doors into the corridor and sliding inexorably down past the front door towards the occupied bedrooms, cresting like a small wave before flowing below the varnished doors and filling the rooms beyond, rising to the meet the blackened roof beams. Mister Jones screamed, the sound echoing through the old house.

Sheila leapt from her bed, the duvet trapping her legs and leaving her thrashing wildly on the floor. She struggled free, climbed to her feet and grabbed at the bedroom door. She pulled it open and stepped out into the hallway. The moon was much higher now in the sky, and silver-bright light lit the corridor clearly. She looked at the end of the hall, and Mister Jones opened his bedroom door and half fell into the corridor. He pulled the bedroom door shut behind him and leant against the outside wall of the house, breathing heavily. Colours were thin in the moonlight, but Sheila could tell that his face was as pale as chalk. He slumped to the floor and she knelt down beside him and took his hand. Mister Jones snatched it back, but she had felt the tremors than ran through him. His breathing was wild and ragged, his chest heaving with the strain of sucking in air.

"What's happened?" Sheila asked. "Was it a bad dream?"

"No dream," managed Mister Jones. "I was awake, wide awake."

"What then?" asked Sheila. She was relieved to see his breathing slow down and become more regular.

"Something woke me up," Mister Jones spoke with some difficulty, his chest still heaving. "Don't know what. Then I felt the bed move as if someone had got in beside me."

"Well it wasn't me!" replied Sheila at once.

Mister Jones turned to look at her, and his eyes looked haunted. "I know, Sheila. I saw a skeleton. Not a living person. And as I looked at it in horror, the skeleton turned its head and looked directly at me!"

"This I must see!"

Mister Jones reached out and grabbed her hand. "No."

"Mister Jones, if there's actually something like that in your room, then we need to know about it!"

"What," replied Mister Jones. "You don't believe me?"

"You were probably still asleep," replied Sheila practically.

"I think I'd rather not go back in there until daylight!"

Sheila regarded her friend dubiously. "There is a spare bedroom, but first, let's see what's in there. I don't fancy going back to bed without being sure you really only had a nightmare."

Mister Jones took a single deep breath and shook his head in an effort to clear it. "Very well. But first, I'm going to get one of the fire irons from the living room. Don't go near that door." Mister Jones got up from the floor, and somewhat unsteadily walked into the living room. He returned a moment later with an iron poker in his right hand. "Cold iron," he said, ignoring the fact that it was still warm to the touch.

"I feel safer already," replied Sheila who had now come to the firm conclusion that he had simply had a very bad dream. There was no sound from the end bedroom. Mister Jones squared his shoulders, and dramatically flung open the door to his bedroom, raising the poker as he did so. The door partly opened, and stuck. Sheila pushed past him and looked around the room. The bed was rumpled and disturbed, the duvet thrown to the floor and blocking the door, but no skeleton, animated or otherwise, could be seen.

"It was there," said Mister Jones slowly, turning on the light. He looked around the whole room, and slowly lowered the iron poker.

Sheila gathered up the duvet and tossed it away from the door in a heap. "Well, it's not here now."

Mister Jones could only nod in agreement.

Sheila gave him a very considered look. "Why don't you use the other bedroom? We've got three."

Mister Jones looked round. "I could, but to be honest I feel a little foolish at the moment, Sheila. It was so vivid I was sure that I was awake, but now..." his voice trailed off.

Sheila took him by the arm, and urged him out of the room.

"You might be better in this one, then." She worked the catch of the other bedroom that lay between those they were using. "Funny, this latch is stuck too."

"Let me try." Mister Jones reached out and attempted to open the door, but the latch seemed to be immobile. "Didn't it work earlier?" he asked.

"Actually, I can't remember. " Sheila tried to recall if either of them had tried to open that bedroom door when they first explored the house, but couldn't remember. She smiled. "But you've given me a great idea for the book, Mister Jones! I'll be able to write something a bit scary in the morning."

"Bet I could do that right now," muttered Mister Jones. Cautiously he put a hand on the door of the end bedroom and it swung open to his touch.

"Don't forget the poker!" said Sheila wickedly.

"I wasn't going to!" Mister Jones, rather reluctantly, stepped through the door and started to rearrange the duvet on his bed.

"Goodnight, then," Sheila called. Mister Jones made no reply, and so she opened her own bedroom door and climbed into the bed. "Didn't think I'd put the duvet back on the bed," she said to herself, but then forgot about that. It was less interesting than the idea of waking up with a skeleton beside you. In fact that thought made her shiver a little, but in a delicious sort of way. She carefully smoothed the duvet down on the bed and checked that her notepad and pencil were in place. And ready to hand if she awoke in what was left of the night with a new idea.

Once again the house was silent. Despite herself, Sheila realised that she was listening carefully in case Mister Jones called out again. After some time, she became dimly aware that she was drifting back into sleep. The duvet was cosy, her pyjamas were warm too. In fact, completely below the duvet, she felt that she was too warm and so she pulled the cover away from her head and let her right arm lie on top of the duvet too beside the pencil and notepad. Sheila sank into a very deep sleep. Although she was hot below the duvet, the temperature of the room began to fall steadily. Her breath became visible as a plume of white air as she breathed in and out in a steady rhythm. Now as she breathed out the vapour turned to ice in the air, and small flecks fell onto the duvet as the room became icily cold. Her right hand twitched.

The rest of the night passed peacefully for me. Perhaps sleeping on one side of the bed with my right hand firmly grasping the iron poker helped in some way. Iron has a singular reputation with occultists I have met, as has silver, in dissuading inimical or hostile things from invading one's personal space, or worse. Waking in the morning light I realised that I had slept longer, or maybe in view of the events of the night I should say later, than was normal for me. I lay still in the bed wondering if I could hear anything from Sheila's room or other parts of the cottage; failing to do so, other pressing demands asserted their requirements on me and I resolved to seek the bathroom without further delay.

In the bright sunlight I felt vaguely foolish holding onto the poker, and I decided to return it to the living room on my way to the bathroom. After all, I might need it to help me clean out the fireplace and lay a fresh fire for the coming evening. I hesitated only briefly before I opened my bedroom door and went down the corridor. Stopping at the entrance to the living room, I went inside and put the poker down on the iron grate. It made more noise than I expected and I looked around guiltily. Sheila did not, however, appear at her door grumbling at me for disturbing her and so I headed for the bathroom.

The moment I touched the latch, a blood-curdling scream made me flinch. I ran at once towards Sheila's bedroom and as she screamed a second time, I didn't hesitate to fling open her door. She was pressed against the wall of her room, as far from her bed as possible. "Sheila? What is it?" I asked.

She didn't reply at first, but with a shaking hand pointed at the bed. I could see nothing amiss. "The pad! The pad!" she gasped.

I picked up her notepad to examine it. As I did so, the remains of a pencil fell onto the duvet; I say remains as the end was splintered and broken. Clearly a great deal of force had been used when on the notepad had been scrawled the words:

HELP ME   HELP ME

I looked round at Sheila. "This?" I asked.

"Yes." She was still shaking, so I dropped the pad back onto her bed and rather awkwardly put my arm around her shoulders.

I thought carefully. "Was that written on your pad overnight?"

Sheila nodded. It was clear even to me that she was crying silent tears of fear, so with my free hand I pulled a packet of tissues from my pocket and gave it to her. She pulled one tissue from the packet and dropped the rest on the floor.

Cautiously I asked her: "Did you - do you - have you any suggestion who might have written it?"

"Yes," she replied. "It's *my* handwriting!" She burst into tears again.

"Tea!" I told her firmly, and led her out of the bedroom, down the corridor and into the living room. When she was safely installed on a sofa I first paid my delayed visit to the bathroom, then went into the kitchen and after filling the kettle, set it to boil. I went back into the living room to see that Sheila had calmed down to the extent that she was now shuffling the papers of plot lines for her novel. "Er, do you want any breakfast?" I asked nervously.

Sheila looked up at me from the sofa with an abstracted air, as if she had only partly heard what I said. I was astonished at how quickly her mood had changed. All the fear had fled from her, and she was engrossed. Rather than disturb her, I walked quickly down the corridor to my bedroom and opened the door without a second thought. I stopped short then, with a frozen memory of last night's visitation; but in the warm morning light, the room was entirely benign and without any trace of last night's horror. My clothes had been scattered somewhat when I reacted to that nightmare vision and as I picked them up and dressed I began to wonder if it had been real, or if Sheila had been right and all along I had been dreaming.

Properly dressed, I walked back down the hallway to the kitchen. The kettle was whistling merrily and I quickly made some hot drinks and took them into the living room where Sheila was still busy with her papers and a fresh pad of notepaper. I was going to place the cups on the coffee table she was using, but she waved me away without even looking up.

"Just over there somewhere please, Mister Jones," she said.

"Sheila? Are you… well, are you all right? I mean a minute or two ago you were quite shocked."

"Oh, I was just being silly, wasn't I? I'd obviously been dreaming and started to make a note on the pad, but forgotten about it afterwards." Sheila put down the sheet of paper she was holding, and looked around. "Ah. Tea. Good." She pounced on the cup and savoured a sip, before pulling a face. "No sugar?" She put down the cup and jumped up from her seat.

"I'll go," I said to her. "You look busy."

"No, I'll go," she said firmly. Sheila walked out of the room. I looked after her in some confusion, how had her mood changed so quickly? Carrying a small bowl full of sugar, Sheila walked back into the living room. She caught my confused expression and smiled. "It's a writer thing, Mister Jones," she said. "We can take our own experiences and work them out on paper." She spooned sugar into her cup, and then returned to her sheets of paper. She picked up her pen, and to all intents and purposes I was alone in the room. I didn't properly understand, but drank some tea to cover that confusion. Then I turned and started to scrape out the ashes from last night's fire.

"What are you doing now?" asked Sheila, sounding annoyed.

"I'm going to get the fire ready for tonight, Sheila, then go for a walk. Leave you in peace to work." I thought that the sooner I was out of her way, the better.

"Oh, right. Thank you, Mister Jones. You sure that you don't mind?"

"Sheila, you arranged this week so that you could have some space in which to write. I was simply going to give you some space to get on with it. It isn't raining, so this is a good day for me to be out of the way, isn't it?"

"Oh, thank you!" Sheila gave me a really bright smile. "I've dragged you out here, and now I'm pushing you out there as well, aren't I?"

"Well, I like walking. It's a bit of a passion of mine, so the chance to walk somewhere fresh is good. Don't think I'll not be enjoying the time, Sheila. I'm very grateful to you for the chance."

Sheila was clearly relieved. "I must admit Mister Jones that I was a bit worried about this aspect of our break."

I smiled at her. "You were very clear about it, so I came here knowing what the score was. It is fine. So I'll be off out, and you can have the house to yourself to work."

"Thank you."

Sheila picked up another sheet of paper from the pile, and I could see her concentrate completely on it and almost forget my presence. I quietly withdrew from the living room. My walking boots and coat were still in my room and so I walked quietly along the corridor. After putting on my outdoor wear, I also took a large-scale local map from my suitcase and carefully fastened it into the map pocket of my walking trousers. I looked into the living room as I opened the front door of the cottage, but Sheila did not even glance up. Her laptop had been turned on and she was totally absorbed in her work. I knew, for she had told me, that the cottage had no internet connection and so I assumed that this would be for her word processor.

Outside, the weather was exceptionally nice. The sky was clear and there was little wind. I did not really need the map, for the path to the cliffs ran straight from the corner of the house, past the window of the bedroom I was using, to the fence beside the Coastal Path. Cheerfully I set out towards the sound of the sea.

*

Sheila sifted through some notes she was holding, then opened the file on her computer that contained her partly completed book. She drew a breath, and closed her eyes for a moment; then she started typing. After some time, she looked at her watch and realised that two hours had passed since her first cup of tea. She saved the document out of habit before putting the laptop to one side and stretching. "Tea!" she said aloud to herself. She walked into the kitchen and put the kettle on to boil. Tapping the worktop with both hands, she paused for a moment before leaving the kitchen for the bathroom. She had not overfilled the kettle and it didn't take long to boil. When Sheila came back into the kitchen it was full of steam. She swore briefly and smiled at herself, for she rarely used bad language. Her recently deceased mother had been very opposed to any swearing and Sheila had therefore never acquired the habit. She poured water onto the tea bag in her cup and peered through the steamed up window. She could see very little through the glass, and shook her head ruefully. She took the bag out of the cup, added some milk from the bottle she had brought with her, and walked back to the living room. Had she looked behind her, she would have been alarmed to see the words **HELP ME** appear briefly in the condensation left on the glass before they faded away.

*

I walked along the path from the cottage until I reached a gate: the gate was unlocked and led directly out onto the Coastal Path that runs along the entire coastline of Wales. In either direction, I could walk for days if I so chose, and that prospect was exciting. However, I also knew that Sheila had asked me to accompany her so that she would not be alone at night and the events of last night in the cottage had made a strong impression on me. Even though I had now mostly convinced myself that I had dreamt what had occurred last night, or what might have happened for there was no evidence to which I could point that in any way demonstrated that my recollection was real, I was sufficiently disturbed not to want to leave Sheila alone in the cottage after darkness had fallen. My limited experience of supernatural things had led me to the conclusion that they mostly operated, or came alive, as it were, after dark.

But this was full daylight, and I had no qualms about leaving Sheila to her writing and taking the chance for some exercise in beautiful scenery on such a lovely day. The choice to be made was; did I turn North or South on the clifftop path? South, I decided, and started out along the bay. I walked very happily for an hour or two, meeting very few people. To my right the sea sparkled in the sun, and I kept a constant eye out for the dolphins and seals that live along this stretch of the coastline. Sadly I was disappointed, and saw neither. The path rose and fell, sometimes dropping down to sea level at wild and unfrequented places before climbing again to some height on the cliff top. Once I walked through a small village where I bought a bottle of water and a sandwich, and resisted the temptation of the rather quaint Fisherman's Inn on the quayside. No commercial fishing boats remained in the small inlet that served as a harbour, just a few pleasure craft that bobbed cheerfully on the rising tide.

At last I decided that it was time to return, and seating myself on a convenient rock I took my Ordnance Survey map of the area out of the special map pocket of my walking trousers. I spread the map wide, then refolded it to let me concentrate on the immediate area. I could see that the coastline had bent outwards in a sweeping semicircle, and although I had walked a considerable distance I was not in fact all that far from Clyffe House. The cottage was not named on the map; but it was clearly shown. Fferm Ffynnon, however, was named and a path that would lead me close to the abandoned farm was well marked on the map. If I struck inland at the next junction of the footpaths and then turned left a quarter of a mile further on, the public right of way would soon take me back. Satisfied, I nodded to myself and holding the map rather than returning it to my pocket, set off.

The next footpath had no gate onto the Coastal Path and also lacked a signpost. I looked at my map briefly, more from habit than anything else, and turned away from the cliff. To my right the Coastal Path ran on and on, vanishing into the far distance and I did feel a momentary desire to follow, to see where it led. With a pang of regret, I walked inland. The footpath was obviously well used, for the ground had eroded quite badly in places and before long I was taking some care how and where I trod. The path wound between stone walls and wire fencing. Many tufts of wool clung to the barbs in the wire, and as the off-shore breeze started to rise they fluttered gently, their movement a distraction at the edge of my sight.

After a mile or so, I stopped and looked at the map. I traced my position as far as I was able and stared across the fields, trying to see the next footpath. I came to the conclusion that it was a little further along and so I walked for another five minutes as the sun slowly began to fall towards the western horizon and the shadows lengthened. Then a badly decayed wooden ladder stile appeared on the wall just ahead of me. I looked at it with some concern. Now about six feet high, the field wall was a little too high to climb easily and the stile itself was poorly, if at all, maintained. Some of the treads had fallen away, and others were very clearly incapable of bearing my weight. For a moment, I debated continuing along the path between the fields, but the fading sunlight encouraged me to return to Clyffe House by the shortest route. I had been out much longer than I had planned already and while I had thoroughly enjoyed my day, I now wondered how Sheila was managing in the cottage. Of course, she herself lived alone in her own home since her mother had died I reasoned, and some solitude was always beneficial. I did not know, but I had always imagined that writing a novel was an activity that required solitude so hopefully Sheila was taking full advantage of my absence.

I grabbed the wooden sides of the stile, and trying to tread as gently as possible I climbed the remaining rungs of the stile. One rung wobbled dangerously but held firm, and I was quickly on top of the wall. I looked out across the field. Fferm Ffynnon was hidden behind a screen of trees, but I was sure that I was in the right place. Gingerly I placed one foot on the topmost tread leading down into the field. It seemed to be strong enough and so I swung my other leg over the top of the wall and touched the rung below. As I transferred my weight both rungs collapsed under my feet, and with broken wood flying around my head, I fell heavily to the ground with a cry and lay clutching my ankle.

*

Clyffe House was a quiet, isolated, place Sheila decided. Both the morning and the afternoon had passed almost unnoticed as she typed. The plan she had crafted for the unfinished part of the novel had lasted only an hour or two, then been torn up and reworked, twice. The screwed up paper she had tossed casually in the direction of the fire. Looking more carefully, Sheila snorted a little as she realised that Mister Jones had not in fact finished cleaning out the ashes from last night's fire, nor laid the preparation for another fire tonight.

"Typical man," Sheila grumbled happily to herself. "Wonder where he's got to? Hope he hasn't got himself lost." With another snort, she tidied up the notes and papers that she had scattered around the living room. Some she tore up or screwed up into a rough ball, others she placed carefully in one of three piles on the side table. When she had finished, she looked out of the window. The view across the fields was pretty, and she enjoyed it for a while. But it was devoid of life, or indeed of a returning Mister Jones, which she suddenly realised she would have liked to see.

The quiet of the cottage was suddenly disturbed by a loud scraping noise and a groan from the hinges of a door. Sheila put her hand to her mouth for a moment, and then laughed at herself. "What is this? A traditional haunted house story?" she said. But a little self-consciously, she picked up one of the fire irons before venturing out into the hallway. To her left, nothing. But when she looked to her right, she was surprised to see that the bedroom door that had refused to open the night before was now ajar. She walked hesitantly down the corridor, and then with a sudden burst of energy pushed the door fully open. She was relieved to see that the room was completely empty. She pulled the door closed and made sure that the latch was shut. She walked back to the living room and dropped the fire iron back by the grate.

The fireplace had a small brush and a small dustpan for removing the ashes. "I wonder where we get rid of them?" she said aloud, suddenly and unexpectedly grateful for the sound of her voice to break the silence in the house. She knelt down and swept about half of the ashes into the dustpan. Taking some care not to spill the ashes and cause herself more work, she stood up and walked out of the living room and into the kitchen. The steam from boiling the kettle had long since evaporated, and after tipping the ashes into the rubbish bin in one corner of the kitchen, she refilled the kettle, placed it on the cooker and switched on one of the heating rings.

"Now, I should think about some food," she said aloud. She had brought a large box of tins and packets of food in the car. "I suppose that I could easily enough drive off to the nearest shop if there's anything I've forgotten," she said, again aloud.

At that, there was a loud crash from the living room and she jumped in alarm. The kettle suddenly boiled with a whistle and she snatched it off the heat, silencing the sound, but not before the boiling steam had obscured the kitchen window. Holding the kettle in her hand, Sheila opened the kitchen door and looked out into the hall. Nothing was there. Nervously she walked into the corridor, and stepped towards the living room. The kitchen door shut behind her with a bang and she jumped again, spilling the boiling water across the wooden floor. Ahead of her, with another groan from the hinges, the far bedroom door swung open.

Nervously she peered into the living room. The fire irons had fallen first into the fireplace, and then seemed to have rolled out across the floor. The remaining ashes were scattered about the hearth, and some still hung in the air. Behind her, the kitchen door slammed again, and Sheila slowly turned around to look back down that part of the long corridor. She went cold as she saw wet footprints leading past her and back towards the kitchen. The prints were made by bare feet, and she looked down at her own feet - firmly encased in slippers. The kitchen door flew open again, banging hard against the wall as it was flung wide. Taking a firm grasp of the kettle, Sheila plucked up her courage and walked to the kitchen door. The steam still obscured the only window into the kitchen, and as she watched the words **HELP ME** appeared again in the steam. She dropped the kettle and fled. At first the front door resisted her frantic attempts to drag it open, then at last it gave way. Sheila half fell outside into the early evening air and staggered across the yard to her car. She collapsed across the bonnet.

"Mister Jones!" she shouted. "Where are you?"

Chapter three

I sat in the empty field, clutching my ankle and wincing with the pain. I looked around, and it was quite obvious that although I had passed other hikers on the Coastal Path, this part of the countryside was much less frequented by walkers. If I did not want to sit by this wall all night, then I was going to have to solve my predicament myself. Grabbing hold of the wall with one hand, and a broken piece of wood with the other, I pushed and hauled myself upright. Gingerly I tried to move my ankle, and with some relief found that I could, although it was very painful.

"Sprained, not broken," I muttered. "Walk it off and it will get better." I was holding a section of wood that had broken away from the side of the stile, and by a lucky chance it would do as a support for my weight. Hopefully the pain would ease as I walked, I reasoned, and so I set off slowly across the field towards the belt of trees on the far side.

Walking slowly and with a little difficulty, I had plenty of time to look around. It was clear that this particular footpath was rarely, if ever, used. Rather than being indistinct, it was non-existent underfoot. However there was a wide metal gate in the wall on the far side of the field, so I made my way towards that. The ground was rough and walking was difficult, even with the help of the makeshift stick. At last I reached the gate, and rested my weight on it with a sigh of relief.

Beyond this wall lay a thin belt of trees, through which I could make out the shape of the farm buildings. This had to be Fferm

Ffynnon, and I was relieved to think that I was now close to Clyffe House. Behind me the sun was sinking lower in the sky, and the air was cool. I shivered. The gate had no lock, but the sliding bolt holding it shut was rusted and would not move. With some difficulty, although my ankle was beginning to feel better after the walk across the field and could almost support my weight again, I climbed the gate and lowered myself gingerly to the floor in the grounds of Fferm Ffynnon.

Immediately there was a change. The air, once cool, now felt cold. The trees, green and welcoming from a distance, now felt dark and intimidating as I walked between them. Brambles lurked amongst the tall grass, ready to catch and trip an unwary or dragging foot. The outbuildings beyond the trees looked forbidding and as I pushed my way through the undergrowth the ruin of the farmhouse rose above them, the empty windows leering down.

I have been unfortunate enough to have had some contact with the supernatural in my past, and I felt once again the sense that something not of our world was nearby. "No," I said to myself. "That's just being silly and melodramatic. You've been watching too many late night horror films." I pushed aside a low-hanging branch and walked beyond the tree line. Immediately in front of me lay a long, low building with a corrugated iron roof. No windows broke the line of the stone wall, which looked grey and forbidding. Brambles and weeds trailed along the side of the building. It felt forsaken and unloved. The wind rose and behind me the trees rustled. I was still unsettled but the quiet, abandoned buildings seemed unremarkable. Beside the left-hand corner of the building was what appeared to be the remains of an overgrown path, so I took that route around the outbuilding and limped towards the old farmyard.

As I rounded the corner, I could see another outbuilding immediately in front of me. The path skirted it. To the right was a further building, or maybe a set of buildings, arranged in an 'L' shape. No doors were visible and all had heavy plywood boards fastened across the windows. I presumed that this was to discourage trespassers, or maybe to stop the young boys of the neighbourhood playing in the old buildings and possibly getting hurt.

The path, such as remained of it, ran along the side of the building in front of me towards the decaying ruin of Fferm Fynnon itself. The sun was now below the treeline, and the bottom part of the old farmhouse was dark, in deep shadow. The crumbling upper story still caught the last of the sun, but the lower half of the building made me feel uneasy. No doubt, I reflected, simply because the air of abandonment and neglect carried its own sadness.

I walked past the old front door of the house and I looked over at the range of outbuildings. The front of the buildings looked as neglected as the rear, but on an impulse I wandered across to the angle of the 'L' shaped building. Perhaps an old milking parlour, I speculated idly. The windows to the front were also boarded up, the plywood boards faded and showing signs of age. As I turned away, I saw a gleam of something white on the floor and looked more closely. It was a cigarette end, and by the freshness of the colouring only recently discarded. Beside it lay a used needle from a syringe and I shook my head sadly. I looked more carefully at the old door. Now I could see signs of recent use. The brambles, nettles, and weeds that grew in such profusion around the buildings did not, in fact, impede the use of this door. The hinges were black, but not pockmarked or speckled with rust; they were new and oiled. Fresh scratches around the keyhole suggested that this building was used, and perhaps at times when the keyhole was hard to see. I put out a hand, and pushed the door; it moved a little, but the lock held fast.

Trespassing was not on my agenda for the day, so I turned away and walked gingerly out of the yard. The gate to the lane was partly open, sagging on the old hinges, and I didn't need to touch it to return to the lane and walk away towards the holiday cottage. Twice I felt that peculiar feeling on the nape of my neck, that primeval sensation of being watched, but although on each occasion I spun quickly around and stared at the old farmhouse, on neither occasion did I see anyone. Before me lay Clyffe House and I quickened my pace, as best I could.

Sheila pushed herself up from the bonnet of her car and looked around the front courtyard of Clyffe House. Then she looked back at the cottage itself, with fear in her eyes. The front door was still open from her flight, but the house itself was still. The lowering sun shone straight through the front door and she could see into the living room. Her laptop was open on the coffee table, and none of the papers appeared disturbed, despite her rapid flight from the building. Understandably, she did not feel inclined to go back inside.

"Where's Mister Jones?" she demanded. "Typical man, never around when he's actually needed!" Trembling, she tried the door to her car. To her immense relief it opened. Sheila scrambled thankfully into the driver's seat and promptly activated the central locking to fasten both doors. She leant back against the headrest, closed her eyes and tried to slow her heart rate.

After a long time, Sheila managed to get some control over her fear. She opened her eyes and stared again into the doorway of Clyffe House. The front door was still open and she could see into the living room. Her papers were undisturbed, and she began to feel that she was being foolish, and worse, cowardly. With a sudden surge of confidence she opened the car door, got out and walked towards the cottage. At once, she could feel that the wind had risen, and was mildly surprised that the front door had not been blown shut. She reached the doorway, and cautiously put one hand on the old timbers. She felt nothing. "Hello?" she called, feeling slightly foolish. Sheila left her hand on the latch and stepped inside the house, looking nervously from side to side. The hallway was empty and the house still silent, so she took a deep breath and - feeling quietly proud of herself - went into the living room.

Despite her having fled from the room in terror, the living room was tidy and her papers and the laptop undisturbed. The remaining ashes in the hearth were piled neatly, ready to be removed. The fire irons were stacked neatly in the hearth. There was no indication that anything at all had taken place to terrify her into leaving the house. In fact, Sheila suddenly began to doubt that she had seen anything frightening. The house was quiet, calm, and even had a friendly atmosphere as the evening sun sank in the sky and the shadows lengthened.

"Tea!" she decided. She wasn't comfortable, alone in the house, and decided that tea would help settle her nerves. Picking up one of the fire irons, she walked into the corridor and then strode firmly into the kitchen. The kitchen too was neat and tidy, the kettle filled and ready to boil. With a hot cup of tea in her hand, Sheila walked back into the corridor that ran the length of the ancient building. She looked down the hall, to the three bedroom doors. Although the sense of fear and threat that had pervaded the house had gone, Sheila did not feel confident to walk down and open any of those bedroom doors. Instead, she went back outside. The sun was well below the tree line, and to the west the old buildings of Fferm Ffynnon were dark against the sky. Sheila hurried to the gate into the lane, and there she could see Mister Jones walking towards her. She waved and he returned the gesture, and then, still limping a little, he quickened his pace towards her.

Reassured and suddenly much more confident, Sheila went back into Clyffe House in a much lighter frame of mind. Suddenly wanting to show her friend that she had been busy all day, Sheila sat down on the couch and turned on the laptop. She cursed under her breath at the slow speed of the computer. "Come on, come on!" she muttered as Mister Jones' feet crunched on some loose stones in the yard near the front door. Finally, the screen cleared and she looked down, expecting to see the desktop screen clearly displayed. Instead, the screen remained a bright blue. In white capital letters the screen read: **HELP ME,** and as Mister Jones appeared in the doorway she opened her mouth to scream.

Leaving the deserted yard of Fferm Ffynnon, I walked down the lane towards Clyffe House. The walking had slowly helped my ankle, and although it still hurt and I was careful not to hurry, and was careful where I placed my feet on the rough ground, I was now able to walk without the makeshift walking stick I had discarded. Some distance away I could see that the lane bent around to the left, and climbed a low prominence. I remembered that the map suggested that our ancient ancestors had built a hill top fort there, and I speculated that the views out over the great sweep of the bay would be magnificent; perhaps that could be my stroll for tomorrow, to keep me out of Sheila's way while she worked on her novel.

At the far end of the lane, another walker appeared. As a small black dog was there too, I supposed that it must be Mr Davis. I was about to wave an acknowledgement when Sheila suddenly appeared in the lane, running out from the entrance to Clyffe House. She was clearly flustered, and waved frantically at me, so I waved back at her. Obviously she was unhurt, so she had not had an accident, I mused. What could be wrong? I quickened my pace and she darted back into the yard, out of view.

As quickly as I could, I walked the remaining yards down the lane and turned into the yard of Clyffe House. The driver's door of Sheila's car was open, and I glanced inside, but the car was unoccupied. Clearly she had gone inside the house; and feeling now in need of more tea and something to eat myself, I followed her. Sheila was sitting on the couch with her laptop open and as I appeared in the doorway she let out a piercing yell.

"Sheila!" I gasped, surprised. "What's the matter?"

Sheila thrust her laptop across the coffee table and jumped up from the couch. She ran across the small intervening space and flung her arms around me. I staggered under the shock and leant back against the wall.

"Mister Jones! I'm so glad you're back!" She held me very tightly.

"Sheila?" I was shocked. We are good friends and neighbours, but our relationship does not normally reach this level of intimacy.

"I've been really scared!" she said, her voice a little muffled as her head was pressed into my chest.

I looked around the room. Apart from her recently discarded laptop, the room was neat and tidy. "Of what?" I asked.

"Look at my laptop!" she replied.

I did so, but could see nothing unusual. "It looks normal to me, Sheila," I replied.

Slowly she raised her head and turned to look at the computer. The screen was quite normal. "That's not what it did when I turned it on," she said in a weak voice.

"I think I'd better make us some tea, and you can tell me all about it," I suggested.

"Fine. Fine. Tea solves everything, doesn't it?"

"Of course it does!" I replied in a light tone of voice. "Hardly anything doesn't look better when you've a cup of tea to drink."

Sheila laughed, in a brittle kind of manner that made me quite worried about her. "Fine. But I'm coming with you." She refused to let go of me and held my arm tightly as we walked somewhat unsteadily down the corridor to the kitchen. Sheila did let go then, and let me walk into the kitchen first. I could tell that the kettle had recently boiled so after adding just a little more water I had made fresh tea for us both in a short space of time.

"Now," I said to her, pushing one mug of hot tea into her hand, "come and sit down and tell me what's been going on. What has scared you this much while I've been out?" I led her by the arm back to the living room. Sheila checked her step at the entrance until I walked in and sat down on one of the two couches. She looked both ways along the hall and then looked at the laptop. Finally she followed me into the living room, and sat down on the same couch: close, but not touching me.

"Clyffe House is haunted," she said. She looked at me with a serious expression, but I wasn't going to disagree; especially after my experience the night before. "When I made no immediate response, she continued. "When you went out this morning, and you forgot to sort out the fire by the way, I wanted to spend the day writing." I nodded, to show that I was listening as much as anything else. "Then," Sheila continued dramatically, "the ghost attacked me!"

I looked at her. She was quite clearly unharmed. "What did it do?" I asked.

"It banged doors and scattered papers!"

I looked around at the neat and tidy room. "In here?"

"Yes, Mister Jones! Everywhere!" Sheila flicked her hair away from her face and gave me a look as if daring me to challenge her. "It must have tidied up afterwards," she admitted. "Also, it has written messages to me, three times."

I put down my cup of tea and half turned so that I could face her. "What messages?" I asked.

"The same message each time. Help me. The last time was on my laptop, when I'd just turned it on." She shifted uneasily on the couch. "That was when I jumped into your arms."

"Good catch, wasn't it?" I asked innocently, and she laughed, breaking the tension she was all too clearly feeling. "Look, Sheila, if the message is 'Help me' then whatever is sending these messages is hardly going to try and hurt either of us, is it?"

"That's too logical for me, Mister Jones. How can you be so logical?"

"Because it helps. So, the question is, what are we going to do now?"

"What do you mean?"

I shrugged at her. "Do we stay or do we go? We can be home in two or three hours drive. If you don't want to stay...?"

That suggestion had a very clear effect on Sheila. From being a little bit frightened, she suddenly became determined and a little bit angry. "I ain't afraid of no ghost!" she said determinedly: then giggled at the film reference, spoiling the effect. "But I wouldn't mind getting out of here for a little bit," she added thoughtfully.

"Tell you what, Sheila, why don't we go out for some food? I'll buy. There was a very nice looking pub in the harbour village I saw earlier."

"That's a good idea!" Sheila was enthusiastic.

"Come on then. We'll go as we are." I walked around the living room, turning on all the lights and lamps as the evening was becoming dark. "I'll turn on the outside lights and the light in the corridor too so that everywhere is bright when we come back."

"Good idea!" replied Sheila. "I'll get my handbag." She suddenly faltered. "It's in my bedroom."

"I'll walk along the passage with you," I told her, and she brightened. When Sheila went into her room, I opened the door to my bedroom and looked around. Nothing had been disturbed, and I closed the door quietly. I switched on the lights in the corridor, and when Sheila came out of her bedroom with a jacket over her arm and her handbag in her left hand, I followed her down to the front door and outside. My last act was to turn on the outside lights that illuminated the yard, so that we would not come back to a dark place that might feel intimidating after our earlier experiences.

"What about the fire?" Sheila asked me as we climbed into her car.

"I'll light it tomorrow night," I told her. "After all, if we stay late in the pub, then we won't need it tonight, will we?"

"Good thinking, Mister Jones," Sheila replied, and drove out of the yard.

Sheila drove through the lanes easily in the twilight that was fast becoming night, and we found the harbour after only a ten minute drive. Sheila parked her car against the harbour wall, with the bright lights of the pub behind us across the car park. For a minute or two we sat in silence, drinking in the beauty of the scene. The tide was flowing into the harbour, the fishing and pleasure boats just becoming afloat and turning on their moorings with the rising waters. "That's really pretty," she said at last, and then spoilt the moment with a loud rumble from her stomach. "Oh! Excuse me!" She put her hand over her mouth in embarrassment.

I chuckled. "Time for food!"

"I hope they are still serving!" Sheila said, and opened her car door. She walked determinedly across the small harbour car park and into the cheerful lights of the pub. Outside were several wooden tables with heavily varnished benches, but Sheila ignored those and headed straight for the bar. By the time I had caught up with her, she had ordered some drinks and was avidly examining the menu. "Bass!" she said to me, knowing of course that neither of us eats meat. "I fancy the sea bass!"

That suited me too, so we ordered two similar meals, and relaxed in the warmth. I looked around the bar; the pub was about a third full. All the customers I presumed would be locals on this night at the end of the holiday season. The locals had obviously assumed we were tourists, but one of them still said hello politely as he approached the bar for more drinks for his friends. Of course, he greeted us in Welsh and smiled when I replied in the same language, before continuing in English.

"Are you two here on holiday then?" he asked.

"Nah," I replied. "My friend here is a writer, here to finish her latest novel. I'm just down to keep her company."

"Oh, right." A couple more of the locals joined us at the bar. "What sort of novel is it, then?" one asked.

"Ghost story," Sheila told them. I was surprised, as she had told me that it was a detective novel she was writing.

"Ghost story! Ha, plenty of those stories round here!" chuckled the first of the locals. We all introduced ourselves, and two of them pulled up bar stools and settled down to chat.

"Where is it you are staying, then?" asked the one who had called himself Emlyn.

"Clyffe House," said Sheila quickly. "Know any stories about that?"

"Which is Clyffe House, then?" asked Emlyn. I was slightly surprised, as I was sure that these men knew the names of every property in the area.

"It's the holiday cottage by Fferm Ffynnon," I answered.

Emlyn frowned, then smiled. "Oh yes, then. The old farm cottage below Caercaddug."

"Where?" asked Sheila.

"The old hill fort. Cadw, the organisation who look after all the Welsh castles and old places, have the care of it. Dylan here can tell you a tall tale or two about the place, I'm sure. For a drink, of course." Emlyn grinned engagingly, and I beckoned to the barman to refill their glasses.

"Not Clyffe House, though?" asked Sheila.

Dylan made a show of draining his glass and passed the empty one across the bar in exchange for a fresh pint. I sighed inwardly and told the barman to put it on my tab with the food.

"Not Clyffe House, no," said Dylan in a deep, musical accent. "But the old fort has been there a long time, and there's more than a few legends there." He took a long drink. "And this village has been a harbour a long time, and where there's the sea there's stories of the long drowned coming back."

"And the hill fort?" asked Sheila.

"Oh, there's stories of the ancient Irish gold traders who would pass along the coast here on their way inland. Not all of them made it of course, and some say that their shades still walk along the lanes on certain nights. And Arthur was here of course, with his men."

"Arthur got everywhere," I muttered.

"So he did, mister," agreed Emlyn. "But see, some of those men from Lampeter University were here some years ago, and they dug up a lot of stuff from the bottom of the hill they said was from that time."

"Ah, right they did," agreed Dylan. "Now, my nan used to tell me that at Samhain, if you stood in the right place, you could see the Old King lead his men out of the hill there for a good old ride around, and a bit of a hunt. But she also said that if they spotted you looking, it would be you that they would be hunting, of course!"

"And then there's the White Lady on the cliffs themselves," offered the barman.

"Aye, can't be forgetting her!" agreed Emlyn.

"What's her story?" asked Sheila.

"Best we let Dylan tell that one," said Emlyn. "He's the best storyteller for miles, round here."

"I do quite a bit of storytelling," explained Dylan.

"That's what your wife says too, bach!" came an unidentified voice from the corner, to a lot of laughter.

"Traditional storytelling," explained Dylan to us when the laughter finally abated. "Tales from The Mabinogion, old legends, that sort of thing."

"Right," agreed Sheila. "I've been to some of the storytelling groups around, so I know how that works." She turned to the barman and signalled that he should draw Dylan another pint of the locally brewed beer.

"Now," started Dylan, "it happened that there was a farmer not too far from here who had two beautiful daughters. Although they had the same parents, the two girls could not have been less alike. One was quiet, and liked helping her mother around the farmhouse, but the younger was a bit wild. She liked nothing more than to be out roaming the fields and the footpaths at all hours and helping her dad with the sheep. As they grew up, both being striking to look at, they naturally had a lot of interest from the local lads." Dylan stopped and drank some beer, while the whole pub waited patiently. Even the cook had stopped work on our food to come out to listen, and I hoped that we wouldn't get a sacrificial offering to eat instead of the bass I was looking forward to.

"Now, the elder daughter, she looked at one or two or more: you have to kiss a lot of frogs, as my mother told my sister," he said to some laughter, "before she made a choice from the boys and moved out to live in her new husband's family's farm. But the younger girl had eyes on higher things. Out walking she had met the son of one of the local gentry and had caught his eye. Now, even though she was beautiful, she was a bit wild and also wasn't well born enough for them days, not to be the wife of a rich man. So the boy's father, he told them to stop seeing each other." Dylan drank again and winked at me over the top of his glass. "Well, he probably didn't say that, but he certainly told his lad that there would be no wedding. I'm sure that you can all tell where this is going, now, can you not? Yes, one night the last daughter had something to tell the boy. The usual thing, she was in the family way. So they saw each other at a lunchtime and arranged to meet in the evening, on the cliffs up there above the harbour, on the headland. The weather was a bit wild and no one knows exactly whom the girl met when she walked the cliff path that night in search of her boy. No one knows where she went over, but the whole village grieved for her the next morning when the boats went out with the tide and found her on the rocks."

Dylan drained his pint of beer. "Now, when she feels it's time, she can be found a walking on the cliff path above the headland there dressed in white and not speaking. It's always a wet night when she's seen, and one or two have slipped on the paths there, themselves, and gone to keep her company." There was some applause, and Dylan smiled. "And her father grieved mightily with the rest and then found that he had lost the heart to work the fields. The farm failed and fell into disrepair and no one now keeps the stead and there's none left now to light the ghost candle in the window, to show her the way home and the way to her rest. Until then, she will walk the cliffs and seek whom she may for some comfort."

Sheila clapped with the others, and Dylan nodded politely before withdrawing to his friends. The cook slipped back into the kitchen, and a moment later came out with a tray of food. "Would you be wanting it at the bar or would you prefer a table, miss?" he asked Sheila. "Oh, a table, please," she replied. "The nearest will do."

The cook set down the plates and then from his tray took some serviettes with cutlery folded inside them, and a small box full of sauces and condiments. "Can I be getting you anything else?" he asked.

Sheila looked at me as I sat down, but I wanted nothing more than to start eating. "No thank you, diolch," she replied. The chef nodded politely and left us to eat. The food was excellent, despite the inattention of the cook while Dylan had been telling his story, and so neither of us spoke for a few minutes. Finally, Sheila swallowed her current mouthful and then put down her cutlery. "What did you think of that story?" she asked me quietly.

I was dismissive. "Very entertaining, but it's an old story, isn't it? You'll hear that tale in a hundred places, with a hundred tiny variations. Here she meets her end on a cliff; inland it will be in a pond or a stream or a river, in other places down a mineshaft or over a steep hillside - whatever is locally to hand, I expect."

"So you don't think it is linked to the haunting? To our haunting? What if it's the ghost of this White Lady asking me to help her?"

"Well, as we are stopping in a house and she's seen on the cliff top path, it seems a bit unlikely, Sheila." I was not keen on Sheila getting some strange ideas about this ghost, especially as

I was sure that she wasn't actually writing a ghost story, and even more especially as I was secretly worried about the coming night in Clyffe House.

"It can't be a coincidence, though!"

"Of course it can," I told her.

"You are no help!"

"Sheila, I'm trying to help. It won't do you any good to get yourself worked up like this."

Sheila glared at me. "Don't you dare accuse me of getting over emotional!"

"Sheila, I'm not. I'm only trying..."

"To be patronising?"

"To get some perspective. It's a ghost story, that's all. Doesn't make it real."

"Next, you will be saying that what I saw today wasn't real," hissed Sheila.

I could not work out why she was suddenly becoming so agitated and angry and said so.

"Well, you'll have plenty of time to work it out on the way back! You're walking!" Sheila grabbed her bag, stood up and flounced off while I sat open-mouthed, looking after her. The small group of locals in the other corner watched her go, and then laughed. I went a bit red in the face with embarrassment.

"Lovers' tiff, is it then?" called Emlyn.

I shook my head. "Is there ever to be any understanding of women?" I asked rhetorically. They all laughed again, and I walked over to the bar. "As I'm walking back, better put a whisky on the bill for me, please," I told him. With a comradely grin, he poured me a measure and put it on the bar. "This is on the house," he told me. I started to thank him, but he waved that away as he took my bank card and fed it into the machine. He gave me the card-reading machine and waited while I entered the security number to authorise the payment for our food. "It's a bit of a tradition, round here," he told me. "Lots of the boys have to walk home after a good night, or maybe a bad one, and if they are good customers then I give them a drink for luck."

"Thanks," I said, taking back my bank card and putting it in my wallet. "It will keep the cold out as I walk back. Have to take the cliff path."

"Then don't stop to chat to any strange women!" called out Dylan, and again all the locals laughed at me.

I waved, and still red in the face walked out into the night. The moon was high now, the clouds thin and scattered. I was still in my walking clothes and shoes, so I had no hesitation in walking to the end of the harbour, and looking out over the sea before turning to my right and starting a slow ascent of the headland. The path was distinct, but had eroded quite badly, and there were many loose stones underfoot. I took my time on the climb, feeling my feet slide occasionally. My ankle still hurt, and I walked slowly and carefully. As I approached the top of the headland, the path became steeper still, and I was glad of the occasional halt to draw breath. There was not enough light for me to refer to my map to see how high the headland rose above the sea level at the harbour, but I estimated it to be at least two hundred feet.

The top of the hill, when finally I reached it, was a wide, grassy triangle. It was immediately obvious that rabbits lived here, from the droppings scattered widely across the closely cropped grass and the several scrapes and holes that were visible even in the poor light. I decided to stick to the path; a short cut across the headland could easily become a disaster if I stepped into one of those traps by mistake or carelessness. I winced occasionally at the twinges from my ankle, but carried on walking as I had little choice.

A thick layer of cloud slipped across the moon, and for a moment the path wavered and became one with the dark surrounding grass. I swallowed, and stepped out more briskly once the light returned, but the clouds were obscuring the moonlight more frequently now for safe walking on the path. I cursed softly as I realised that my torch was either in Clyffe House or in Sheila's car: and in neither case accessible to me now, when I had need of it. The path wound on, closer now to the cliff edge. To my right the ground ceased to be scrubland and a low wall, topped with barbed wire appeared. The base of the wall was rough, the ground uneven and strewn with weeds and trailing brambles, and against my desire I had to walk closer still to the left side of the path - and the precipitous edge of the cliff.

Occasionally I passed through gates, each one bearing a distinctive and unmistakable warning to keep away from the cliff edge, for fear of falling to an early doom; the legend, 'Danger of Death', seemed quite superfluous as the hungry sea at the bottom of the cliff made its presence known. The wind tugged at my jacket and I looked ahead for the gate in the side wall that would lead to Clyffe House. The bushes beside the wall grew higher and obscured my view, then briefly extended along the cliff edge so that I was walking through a tunnel of brambles and foliage. When I finally emerged from the tunnel, my steps faltered. There, a hundred yards ahead of me on the path and walking slowly away from me in a northerly direction, was the dim shape of a woman in white.

I pulled up short, and my breath rattled in my throat. It was impossible not to think of the story told in the pub. The woman, for the wind whipped her dress about her body and clearly she was a woman, continued to walk away from me. I went on then, trying to quicken my pace. Although that might me bring me closer to the apparition; I knew that the path to Clyffe House lay to the north and I felt an urgent desire to get off that windswept cliff path. The loose stones and rough ground made me stumble. I stepped inadvertently to my left; and a small group of stones at the edge of the path rolled over the nearby cliff edge and vanished down into the sea roaring in the darkness below. I dropped to my knees and grasped at the bushes below the wall with my right hand. I swallowed. That could so easily have been me; that could so easily still be me if I lost concentration. I watched my feet carefully for a minute or two as I strode out again; and when I looked up, the woman ahead had gone. The path was empty.

I was starting to limp again now as my ankle still pained me. I rounded a small inlet, the Coastal Path still running close to the edge of the cliff, and there before me was the gate I sought. With a gasp of relief, I pulled the gate open, almost fell through it and closed it behind me. At once I felt safer, and I knew that a danger had been averted. To the north, the trees swayed in the strong breeze, and the clouds scudded across the sky. The Coastal Path looked bleak and mysterious. I looked along the path, expecting to see the lights of Clyffe House beckoning me with the promise of shelter. But all was dark.

Sheila started the car and swung it round in reverse, away from the harbour wall. "How dare Mister Jones patronise me in that way, and spoil the evening," she thought. She was almost surprised at herself to find that she was crying and decided it must be anger. There was no romantic aspect to their friendship, so why did she feel so emotional if it wasn't anger? Without stopping the car, her left hand delved deep into the bag she had thrown onto the passenger seat, and plucked out a tissue. She wiped her eyes, and drove faster along the dark lanes. The now damp tissue she pushed back into her handbag. It must be anger, she decided. Why else would she have made Mister Jones walk back after he had sprained his ankle earlier in the day? That was not like her, not at all.

The wind howled and pushed at the car, and with a start Sheila realised that she had been driving too fast for the lane she was using. A sharp corner sprang out of the darkness at her and she wrenched at the steering wheel with a sob of dismay. The car slid, and slammed into the grass verge, bouncing over the rough and muddy ground. Still sliding, now sideways, Sheila saw a tree loom out of the night. Again she wrenched at the steering wheel and felt the car respond. She closed her eyes and waited for the impact.

The rear of the car struck the tree and the whole car shook before sliding across the grass and back onto the road. Shaken,

Sheila stopped and climbed out to look at the damage. Immediately the wind seized her long hair and blew it across her face, so that she had to hold it back with one hand while she peered at the car. She could see very little in the darkness and had to wait until the gathering clouds let some fitful moonlight pass. The car seemed to be dented, but driveable, and she let out a loud gasp of relief. Back in the driver's seat she let in the clutch and drove away much more sedately. However, it was clear that there was some serious damage as the car travelled unevenly, and there was a most unpleasant sound from the back wheel.

"Please let me get back to the cottage!" Sheila prayed aloud. The turning to Fferm Ffynnon and Clyffe House arrived at last and she turned gratefully down the lane. Still jolting and squealing, the Peugeot kept moving forward. When she passed the looming ruin of Fferm Ffynnon, Sheila fixed her gaze ahead. The clouds parted and at the end of the lane she could see the dark bulk of Caercaddug, the ancient hillfort. Lights flickered mysteriously on the side of the hill, but then her attention was drawn to the entrance to the yard of Clyffe House. She turned the protesting Peugeot into the yard and thankfully turned the engine off.

"Wait a moment," she said aloud. "We left all the lights on when we went out!" She looked nervously at the long, low building. Clyffe House lay in darkness, even though many lights had been left burning when they set out for the pub. Sheila decided that she was too nervous to approach the cottage on her own, and wondered where Mister Jones was. Now she really regretted her sudden outburst and wondered again what had caused it.

Sheila looked nervously at the dark house. There had to be a simple explanation. After some time, feeling that she was being foolish by just sitting there, she got out of the car. Exasperated at herself she approached the door; but when it came to it, she found that she lacked the courage to enter the holiday cottage. Upset and disgusted with herself she walked to the yard gate and looked up and down the lane in the hope of seeing Mister Jones approaching again. There was no one on the lane. But when she looked to the left, down towards the old hillfort, once again she could see flickering lights on the side of the hill.

"Pretty," she said to herself. Then as she watched, the lights started to move, rising up the side of the hill at an oblique angle, before reaching the top and vanishing. The line was not long, and soon they had all passed out of sight. She turned away from the lane, and with a cry of relief saw Mister Jones limping around the side of the cottage and crossing the yard. She ran across the yard, and once again threw her arms around him.

"Whoof!" said Mister Jones, intelligently.

"I'm sorry, Mister Jones, I'm sorry!" Sheila half sobbed, holding him tight.

Mister Jones looked rather uncomfortable. "Sheila? Are you all right? And why have you turned all the lights off?"

"I didn't. They were all turned off when I got here."

Mister Jones managed to detach himself from Sheila and look curiously at the cottage. "Who turned them off then?"

"How should I know?" asked Sheila, her confidence returning now she was no longer alone. "Why don't we go and see?"

"All right." Mister Jones hesitated a moment, then walked up to the front door. He hesitated again, then opened the door and stepped inside. The door swung shut behind him, and Sheila caught her breath. Nothing happened for a minute or two, and she began to shake. But then the lights flooded on inside, the bright light flooding through the windows into the yard. A moment later the outside lights came on too, and then the front door opened. Mister Jones stood there unharmed, and Sheila released her breath with relief.

"The main fuse box had tripped. Nothing alarming," Mister Jones' voice was calm and reassuring. He held the door open and Sheila walked into the cottage with some caution. She looked around the living room; but it was undisturbed, and she relaxed a little.

"I've had an accident," Sheila said.

Mister Jones looked alarmed. "Are you hurt?"

"No, but my car is damaged."

"Oh dear. Well, we can sort that out in the morning. I had a strange experience on the way back here."

Sheila wasn't very interested. "Tell me in a while. Better still, in the morning. I'm still a little shaken, Mister Jones, and I'd rather settle down. Were the lights really only off because of the fuse box?" She sat down on a couch and looked at her laptop. She decided not to turn it on.

"Oh yes. The main switch had tripped out for some reason. I reset the switch and the lights came back on at once." Mister Jones walked down the hallway towards the kitchen. "I'm going to make tea. Do you want some?"

"Could I have a coffee, please?"

"Won't it keep you awake?" Mister Jones called from the kitchen.

"I hope so," Sheila muttered. Outside the wind became stronger and made small sounds in the eaves of the cottage.

"Tell me about the accident, then?" asked Mister Jones, coming back into the living room with two mugs and a packet of biscuits.

"Nothing really. I was just going a bit too fast for these lanes and didn't take a corner properly. I bumped into a tree, and now there's a horrid noise from the back of the car." Sheila shivered and drank some coffee gratefully.

"It's lucky you got back here, then! Why didn't you come inside when you got back?"

Sheila looked down into her cup. "The lights were out, and I was too nervous."

"I can understand that," said Mister Jones. "I was a bit nervous myself as I walked across the fields from the Coastal Path and the house was so dark. What did you do then?" As he spoke all the lights flickered off, and came back on again.

Sheila looked nervously all around the room. "I sat in the car for a while. Then I got out and thought about coming inside, but first went down to the lane to see if you were coming that way." She didn't want to admit that she was too frightened to go inside Clyffe House. "But one odd thing I did see."

"What was that?"

"Down the lane that way," - Sheila pointed towards the hillfort - "I saw a line of lights go up and over the hill and then go out."

Mister Jones shrugged. "Walkers, I expect."

"At this time of night?"

"Some people like walking in the night. I do sometimes. Or it could have been boy scouts or something like that."

Sheila nodded. "I suppose so. It just looked odd, that's all." She drank some more coffee and took a second biscuit. "Are you going to light the fire?"

Mister Jones looked at the ashes still in the hearth. "Do you want me to?" The lights went out again.

"Yes!" said Sheila firmly. "I do not want to be in here with no lights! And there's nowhere else we can go now, not with the car broken."

Mister Jones turned to face the hearth, and knelt down. There was a loud crash.

"What was that?" demanded Sheila.

"Sorry, I knocked the fire irons over." The lights came back on but flickered off and on constantly. The wind began to make loud moaning noises around the cottage and Sheila looked very unsettled. Mister Jones gathered up the remaining ashes in the dustpan and took them to the bin in the kitchen. Returning to the living room he gathered together a pile of small pieces of wood to use as kindling, and lit a white firelighter brick under them. The bright flames from the firelighter quickly set the kindling alight and Mister Jones added more wood to the blaze.

The lights went out again.

"The joys of having a rural property, I suppose," Mister Jones said. "Power problems must be a regular hazard." He added some more substantial wood to the fire and sat back on a couch. The lights stayed off.

"Would you check the fuse box again?" asked Sheila in a brittle tone.

Mister Jones looked at her. The firelight was not bright enough for him to see her expression clearly, but he had realised from her tone that she was nervous and unhappy about this darkness. "Of course," he said, and made his way out of the living room. He groped his way slowly into the kitchen and opened the fuse box on the wall. "It's not the fuses this time," he called back. "It must be a problem with the mains power. We'll report it in the morning if it isn't back on."

"And what do we do overnight?" demanded Sheila.

"Sleep?" suggested Mister Jones, coming back into the living room.

"Well, I'm staying here!" announced Sheila.

"Don't you think you'd be more comfortable in bed?" asked Mister Jones.

"I don't feel very safe," replied Sheila in a small voice. "I'd rather be with you."

"Er…"

"Oh, I don't mean like that!" replied Sheila at once. "I'd just rather that we both stayed here in this room, where there's the fire. Are there any candles?"

"I couldn't see any. And it's too dark for a proper search."

"Doesn't matter. Build the fire up a bit, and that will do."

Mister Jones added some chopped up logs to the fire and the light from the hearth died. Sheila shivered.

"Shall I get you a duvet?" Mister Jones asked her.

"Would you mind?"

"Not at all. In fact, if we are staying in here tonight, I'll get one for myself too." Mister Jones left the living room and headed off down the corridor. The flames rose again in the hearth around the newly added wood, and Sheila relaxed in spite of the eerie noises the wind was making outside. A shower of rain hit the windows of the living room in a sharp burst of noise and she flinched.

Mister Jones returned with a duvet in his arms. "I could only carry one at a time," he said. "This one's yours." He gave Sheila the duvet and she gratefully spread it out over herself as he walked back out of the living room. She heard Mister Jones walk firmly down the hallway and then heard him open his bedroom door. She snuggled down on the couch under her duvet, feeling warm and comfortable and watched the flames in the hearth. She waited for what seemed an age but there was no sound of Mister Jones returning down the corridor, and she began to feel uneasy. A log shifted in the hearth, the flames rose and fell and sparks flew across the room. She watched their flight until they had all extinguished and wondered where her friend was. When the fire was fading and he still had not returned, Sheila was torn between emotions; she was angry at Mister Jones for leaving her on her own when she had asked him not to and worried in case something was preventing his return to the living room. Either way, she did not want to be alone that night. Rain hammered again on the windows and then passed on. She shivered, even under the warm duvet.

At last, she screwed up her remaining courage and thrust the duvet to one side and got up from the couch. Her bag fell to the floor, scattering its contents, but she ignored it. Sheila added more wood to the fire and picked up the iron poker from the hearth. Cautiously she walked down the corridor towards the bedrooms. Her bedroom door was slightly open. She pushed it hard with the poker and it swung back, wide. The crash as it hit the wall made her jump. She looked into the bedroom, but it was empty. The bed was bare of a duvet as she had expected. Sheila stepped back from the door and turned towards the end bedroom. She knocked on the door and called out, but there was no reply. She tried the latch; but it would not move. Panicking slightly, she pushed hard at the latch, and still it was immobile. She called Mister Jones' name again, quite loudly - there was no reply. She pressed both hands against the latch. Whether it was the extra strength from her using two hands, or the sudden touch of the iron poker against the latch was unclear; but it moved without resistance and the door swung open. The duvet remained in place on the bed, and there was no sign of Mister Jones in the room.

Chapter four

The wind in the treetops was becoming fierce, and a hint of rain was in the air. Instinctively, the small group of men and women clustered together by the gate in the field wall turned their backs to the weather.

"Who's late, then?" demanded Iuan Davis.

"Idris, Iuan. He had to lock up the pub; we set off before him."

"He'll miss out if he's much later." Mr Davis looked at his watch. It was hidden under a long sleeve, and he shook his arm irritably to free his wrist from the cloth.

"He's coming now." One of the women present pointed across the fields towards the Coastal Path. A powerful torch was lighting the way for the publican who was clearly walking as fast as he could in the darkness.

"Right," said Iuan Davis with authority. "Megan, light the torches, please."

The lady who had spoken earlier turned to a brazier hidden behind the stone wall and lit the fire laid in it. It blazed quickly, and she nodded in satisfaction. Then she picked up a sports bag that lay next to the brazier and opened it. Inside were eight long pieces of wood, each with a metal cage at one end. The cage was filled with wood and resin, and wrapped in plastic. One by one, Megan thrust the cages into the brazier which promptly gave off a noxious black smoke as the plastic burned away.

"Let's go," instructed Mr Davis. "Idris can catch us up, leave his torch burning." He took the end of one of the poles and lifted the burning end out of the brazier. Sparks flew off into the night, and the others turned their faces away to avoid the embers. They too took their burning brands from the brazier, which now started to die down as the fuel in it was exhausted. Mr Davis set off along the well-kept path that led up the side of the hill towards the top of the ancient fort. One by one the others fell in behind him and the line of torches began to rise as they climbed. Behind them the wooden gate banged shut twice. First in the wind, then a second time as Idris hurried through the gate, panting for breath. He shrugged off the long rainproof coat he was wearing and thrust it down below the now empty sports bag against the stone wall. He picked up a convenient large stone and dropped it on the bag to stop both things from blowing away if the weather became much worse. Then he grabbed his burning torch and hurried up the winding path to catch his friends and comrades as they climbed in a stately, measured procession.

Deep ditches, part of the old fortifications, ran around the top of the hill in concentric circles. Iuan Davis turned off the path and plunged into the deepest ditch, walking widdershins around the fort. The others followed, treading carefully now that the track was less well kept and uneven under foot. Indeed, it was clear that they were the only ones to pass this way on this lonely, desolate and almost remote hilltop. Close to a stone that stood on the outside wall of the ditch, Mr Davis pulled at a large bush that grew against the hill, and it fell aside. A small opening was revealed, dark even against the dark grass. Mr Davis raised his burning torch, and one by one the others filed past him into the hill itself. Mr Davis entered last. Going before him, the torches carried by the others had taken a red light into the hillside. He strode easily along a short passage, then down a long flight of stone stairs and finally entered a large cavern deep within the hill.

Those who had preceded him were now filing around the chamber. The very centre of the cave held a round pool of water. At one point the otherwise perfect circle was interrupted by a set of steps that led down into the depths. Beside the steps was set a huge, ornately carved chair, in truth a throne, wrought in ancient times from a dark wood. An aura of age, unfathomable age, lay about it. The carvings were strange and seemed to twist and move in the flickering light from the wooden torches. Around the rim of the pool was set a wide painted circle full of strange images and symbols of an esoteric and occult design. The throne was so set as to look out across the dark pool and form an integral part of the design: despite its antiquity the paint still shone in bright colours. Iuan Davis waited until his comrades had stopped at equidistant points around the circle before walking slowly to the top of the steps. They all raised their torches aloft and began to chant the word 'Addanc' over and over again. The cave filled with the echoes of the word and their voices became louder and louder.

Now the whole chamber was filled with the sound, which was almost anxious or entreating in its tone. Suddenly the placid waters of the pool shivered. Ripples started in the very centre, and spread outwards to the edge of the pool, gathering in frequency. The chant now rose louder, in triumph:

"Addanc, Addanc, Addanc, Addanc, Addanc. *Addanc, Addanc, Addanc, Addanc, Addanc - ADDANC, ADDANC, ADDANC, ADDANC, ADDANC, ADDANC, ADDANC!*"

At the last cry, which reached an almost orgiastic pitch, a sharp point pierced the very centre of the pool. This continued to rise and slowly reveal that it was the crest of the head of an ancient nightmare, by some freakish chance still alive in modern times. The long snout opened slightly to reveal rows of teeth. The nostrils opened and distended to allow the ingress of air rather than water and the hooded and crested eyes glared around the chamber at those awaiting the Addanc's return from the depths.

"*ADDANC, ADDANC, ADDANC, ADDANC, ADDANC!*" They cried, dipping their torches in homage.

Still the Addanc rose, revealing that the monstrous and alien head was frighteningly and disturbingly set upon the shoulders and body of an adult male human - but a body twisted and distorted, lumpen and misshapen with overlong arms and webbed fingers.

"*Addanc, Addanc, Addanc, Addanc, Addanc!*" The chant lowered in volume, became softer and reverential.

Still the Addanc rose from the depths, its head twisting around the chamber, examining those present. Satisfied, it set its feet upon the stone stairway and dripping water and coated with a green slime; it stepped free from the pool. It turned to survey those who had summoned its presence, its eyes glittering with malevolence and distaste. Iuan Davis spread his arms wide and bowed before the creature. The others followed his lead, and then as one, they all sank to their knees and threw back the hoods that had previously hidden their faces. The pockmarks that distinguished and marred Mr Davis' forehead and cheeks were also mirrored on the others' faces and it could be seen that they were all merely a pale imitation of the scales and marks on the head of the Addanc. The ancient monster turned around once and then slowly, regally, took its seat on the throne.

"Maester, we are here," said Iuan Davis.

The Addanc glared around the chamber and then spoke. Its voice was soft, with liquid consonants but somehow conveyed a menace and held the chill of the deep waters of the earth where the sun never reaches.

"Few, so few now to my worship."

"Maester," acknowledged the remaining followers, in one breath.

"Why have you not done as I instructed and brought more to this ancient hallowed place?" demanded the Addanc. "Why have so few others been sent to meet me in recent times?"

Iuan Davis was pale. "Maester, these are new times. Men are harder to turn to the Old Ways."

The Addanc regarded him curiously. "Yet you return here at this time of the year."

Davis bowed. "As we must, to receive your gift, Maester. The gift of life for another season."

"Ah, yes, my gift to you. To you all, so few now, despite my wishes. Despite my commands. Despite my desires."

Mr Davis did not care to reply.

"My desires mean so little to you now?" asked the Addanc. "You desire your life so little now?"

"Maester, we desire your life," all repeated in unison.

"Perhaps, this time, I will not grant you my gift."

"Maester, tell us what we must do to please you," groaned Megan.

The Addanc stood. It paced around the pool, looking at each of the kneeling worshippers. Carefully it avoided the outer edge of the painted circle, where the bright painted letters of an ancient and forgotten language ran, words in a tongue that had died long before the Romans ventured to the shores on a misty and mysterious island at the furthest extent of their known world.

"So, I have pondered long on this matter." The Addanc continued around the circle, leaving wet footprints behind in its path. "It seems to me that the time has come for me to emerge again, and take my rightful place in this world; and for you, my loyal acolytes, so few now in number, to be my agents, to be my messengers, to be my weapons as well as my guardians and devotees."

Iuan Davis raised his head as the Addanc stopped before him.

"Go to my altar," instructed the Addanc.

Iuan Davis stood up and looked over to the far corner of the chamber. The Addanc waved an arm in a casual motion and several candles set into sconces on the wall behind and to either side of the altar burst into life. Slowly Davis walked to the altar and sank to his knees before it.

"On top you will see a manuscript. Open it. Turn to the fortieth page."

Davis did as instructed and bending over the low stone altar carefully turned the brittle pages of the ancient book. Several of the painted images he saw on the pages excited him; others made him shudder. He counted the pages as he turned them, and stopped on the fortieth page.

"There will you find a list of the things I require you to bring to the chamber. Tomorrow night you will attend me again. Tomorrow night will be the start. Too long have I slumbered while this world turned." The Addanc stepped back into the pool. Several of its worshippers groaned in dismay, and the Addanc swept them all with a cold gaze. "Fear not. Fear not. That which I desire shall come to pass, and then you shall all receive your due. You shall all share in my plan. Attend! Be here tomorrow night without fail."

The Addanc stepped down into the pool, and slowly slid below the dark waters, the crest on the top of its head being the last part to slip from sight. The ripples spread outwards from the centre of the pool to the very edge where the devotees remained motionless upon their knees, and slowly, so slowly, stilled. The pool was without motion when at last Iuan Davis rose to his feet, and cast the hood back over his head.

"Same time tomorrow, then," he said in a conversational tone.

"Iuan," started one of the men.

"Morgan, this is not the time or place. Our Maester has spoken; it is to us now to do his bidding."

Davis straightened his back, and started to walk towards the passageway to the outside. The others fell in slowly behind him, and followed him from the chamber. As they left the waters of the pool rippled again. Without ceremony, the Addanc rose silently from the pool and sat on the throne. His gaze turned to the far altar that was still lit by the candles on the wall, and he stared at it without moving, his expression alien and unfathomable. The flicker from the torches in the passageway died. The candles were the only source of light in the still chamber as the Addanc thought and pondered -and planned.

I walked along the dark corridor to my bedroom and tried to lift the latch on the door. To my considerable surprise, it would not move. I recalled Sheila being unable to move the latch yesterday, but for me it had opened easily. I was confused, rather than alarmed. I pressed down hard on the latch, and then lifted it with all the force at my command; the latch still did not move. I stepped back and regarded the door. There was no fastening on the latch; nothing that would stop it moving, nothing to stop it opening. I tried again with no more success than before.

Confused, I put out my right hand and leant against the wall. But my hand didn't touch the wall; instead I pushed against the door of the bedroom we were not using and that door swung open without a sound. With no lights in the building the room was very dark. I was unwilling to enter at first and again tried the latch to my own bedroom door. Still it refused to open. I did need a duvet for the night though and so decided to get the duvet from this third bedroom. Swallowing nervously I stepped through the door and felt around in the strange room for the bed. Some light came through the single window as clouds were driven across the sky and let some moonlight filter down. Dimly

I could see across the room to the bed against the far wall, but the floor was in shadow. I walked towards the bed, my hand stretching out for the duvet as the moonlight failed. But instead of reaching the bed I suddenly felt the floor tilt beneath my feet. With a gasp - I had no time to call out or shout - I lost my balance and fell. I found that I was on a steeply sloping floor and slid down into a deeper darkness than I had met thus far in Clyffe House.

When I stopped sliding, I was in absolute darkness sitting on a level floor. I reached out with both hands and discovered quickly that I was in a passageway five feet high, and about three people wide. The slope down which I had entered this passage was behind me, and I tried to go back up it to get back into Clyffe House itself. Before long it became obvious that the gradient was too steep for me to climb successfully. Using my hands, I tried to find the hole in the ceiling at the top of the slide, but my hands encountered only the solid rock of the tunnel roof. I shouted for Sheila as loudly as I could, but the echoes of my cries ran away down the tunnel, and I came to the gloomy conclusion that I was unlikely to be rescued from above. The tunnel led away in two directions. There was no way of my knowing what lay at either end and so with a sinking feeling in my stomach I made a choice and followed it.

After just a moment, I stopped. I had bumped my head badly on the low roof and perhaps it had knocked a little sense into me. It certainly hurt. I sat down on the floor of the tunnel, and rubbed my head ruefully. But what about Sheila? I knew that she was nervous to the point of terror about being in Clyffe House alone, and now it was after nightfall and the power had failed. She was alone, in a house that she believed, with good reason, I was prepared to admit, to be haunted. She was alone, scared, and without the support of another person. I had a duty to try and get back into the house, I decided. Now, how was I to achieve this?

I could go on down this tunnel, and see where it led. That was a possible option. But in my limited knowledge of tunnels, they led from one place to another, often over some distance. The likelihood of the tunnel ending in Clyffe House was very slim, I reasoned. Right: so where else might it end? Below ground I had no way of knowing which direction I was going. The tunnel might go to Fferm Ffynnon; a strong, if unpleasant possibility, but at least I could walk back to Clyffe House in a reasonably short time. Or it might go somewhere else, somewhere unknown. Maybe some considerable distance away.

The most sensible thing, I decided, was to have another attempt at climbing back into the cottage. I had probably given up on the attempt too early, I decided, and should try again before heading off down a tunnel of unknowable length to an uncertain destination. So I turned around and crawled my way back up to the end of the tunnel. There was the steep slope down which I had fallen. I reached out, and with my hands tried to determine exactly how wide and steep the slope was. Realising that I did not have to stay on my knees, I stood upright and stretched my back, then reached upwards as high as I could. The top of the slope was, of course, the roof of the tunnel and around the top of the slope the roof felt different. In a moment of inspiration I took off one shoe and reached upwards to hit the ceiling, or the floor of the bedroom from which I had tumbled. I hit the roof of the tunnel or perhaps the trapdoor through which I had fallen with the heel of the shoe; it struck something with a dull thud and fell back to the floor of the tunnel. I had a momentary panic when I couldn't find the shoe in the darkness. I dropped to my knees, and cast my arms out all around me; with a small sob of relief, a sob of which I was instantly rather ashamed, I put my hand on it and quickly shoved my shoe back onto my foot.

So the slope now had a ceiling. That could only be the floor of the third bedroom, now restored to its normal place, I reasoned. In some way I must have inadvertently triggered a trapdoor, and fallen into a hidden tunnel. Perhaps a smuggler's tunnel from centuries ago? In which case it wasn't going to come out at Fferm Ffynnon, I thought, but somewhere further away. I tried shouting Sheila's name, but the echoes just ran along the tunnel and faded into the distance. Reluctantly I came to the conclusion that no help was going to arrive from above and that I was going to have to try and escape on my own, and that meant using the tunnel.

My choices were limited: did I crawl along the tunnel or crouch? Neither appealed much. So in the end, I set off with my head bent low. I held one hand in front of me with the fingertips brushing the roof of the tunnel in case I met any low hanging rocks or unevenness that could cause my headache to get worse. It was too dark to see my watch, and already my sense of time passing had gone. I no longer knew how long I had been trapped underground and my distaste for the tunnel was rising. I sat down and leant against one wall. My fear of being trapped down here rose to a pitch, and to my horror I turned to one side and was violently sick. There was a strange sound, and I listened to it for a moment before realising I was hearing the echo of myself sobbing. That was as frightening as my situation and I resolved to get a grip on myself.

Struggling back to my feet I set off again down the tunnel. After walking for an age, I stopped for a rest. Then I wondered how it was that the air seemed so fresh? All that I had ever read about tunnels and mines suggested that fresh air was a big issue when underground, yet in this tunnel I was having no such problem. Had those who delved this built air vents into the design? Or was there an opening to the air at the end? Either thought gave me renewed optimism for it reminded me that the tunnel was not unending, and that it had been made for a purpose. Still stooping, I walked on with renewed vigour. I then thought about all the adventures in tunnels I could remember. The Minotaur in his labyrinth. Adventurers in the catacombs of Rome; the films of Indiana Jones; at least those had turned out well for him! Although I strongly suspected that I was less able to cope than that other Mister Jones if faced by poisoned darts or blockages in the tunnel. I quickly dismissed that thought as being unhelpful. What else? The prisoners who had dug tunnels in World War Two, in order to escape? Briefly I recalled the scenes from The Great Escape. One of the Alien films had Sigourney Weaver in a tunnel with a horrid alien pursuing her, I remembered; that thought too I quickly dismissed. Finally, I thought of Bilbo Baggins descending the long tunnel in a mountain to meet a dragon. Perhaps that was horribly more pertinent, I thought. With a shiver I carried on walking for, like Bilbo, I had no choice.

The tunnel continued on. It was quite straight and I found no turns or side passages. For the latter I was grateful; I have sometimes had nightmares about being lost underground in a maze of passages. I knew how well-prepared adventurers coped with mazes and tunnels; I had none of the essentials they carried as a matter of course. My back hurt where I had to stoop because of the low roof, but I pressed onwards. I have no idea how long I walked, or staggered, along that tunnel. It could have been hours, or a matter of minutes; but eventually it came to an end. There was no light as such, no brilliance or welcome daylight, but a faint reddish glow suddenly appeared on the floor and on one wall ahead of me. I stumbled forward gladly, and then halted as caution arose within me. I walked as softly as I could toward the red glow. Was I, like Mr Baggins, about to encounter a dragon?

The end of the tunnel curved abruptly to the right before ending, either by design or because the ancient miners had miscalculated. I stopped at the corner and peered cautiously around at what I hoped would be the exit. The tunnel narrowed to a small doorway, from which on ancient and decaying hinges hung the remains of an oaken door. The door, which was splintered and warped, hung open at an angle and allowed the light that was causing the glow to penetrate the mouth of the tunnel. Suddenly I was desperate for some water, not least to clear the sour taste of vomit from my mouth and throat.

Satisfied that I could approach the doorway without revealing myself, I crept as quietly as I could around the corner of the tunnel and then peered through the remains of the door. I could see into a large cave and was immediately disappointed that the tunnel had not led me out into the open air. The chamber was lit by a reddish light, from some source outside of my line of sight. I could see a round pool of water in the centre of the room and dimly make out something painted on the floor around the pool. Some sort of decoration I presumed. Beside the pool stood a large chair covered with ornate carvings. I peered around as best I could, but the chamber appeared to be completely empty. However, not far away from me, I could see another opening in the wall and hoped that this other passageway might be a way out, a way to safety, a way to return to Clyffe House.

I listened carefully, but no sound disturbed the brooding silence of the chamber. As gently as I could, I eased the remains of the door open and stepped down into the chamber. Immediately I looked around. The light came from behind a low altar: four huge candles burned from sconces fixed to the wall. I could see a huge book and various objects on the altar; but I felt no inclination to wait and examine them. Instead, I stepped softly towards the other passageway. A cold wind blew down the passage, and my hopes rose as I went into it. Again it was dark but on the floor were some stray leaves and an occasional broken twig. I stepped on one twig and the crack as it broke underfoot nearly stopped my heart. I understood that I had reached the end of the passage when my outstretched arms were badly scratched by an encounter with a thorn bush. In a panic I pushed hard, ignoring the pain, and the bush fell away. I waited, looking out through the rough doorway. Moon shadows chased themselves across the ground outside and in the moving shadows I fancied I could see the shape of a still and silent sentinel. Had I made my way through that long darkness only to be captured at the moment of freedom? Gritting my teeth, I stumbled out of the dark passage into a dark night on an open hillside, and made my way over the uneven ground away from that awful passageway, as swiftly as I could. I was alone. The sentinel was a standing stone. The thorn bush lay to one side of the narrow entrance to the depths of the hill, and I staggered away from it with a cry of relief.

The moon shone out clearly as the clouds were blown away for a moment, and I could see my way down from the hilltop. I realised that I was on the old hillfort, and with a start recognised the long, low, shape of Clyffe House some distance away. Beyond that lay Fferm Ffynnon. Lights flickered there amongst the ruins, and I felt a deep chill that had nothing to do with the cold wind at my back.

The hillside rose and fell unevenly, but then I found a well made and repaired pathway leading down the hill. Clearly the track was well used, as in the brief moments of moonlight I could see the marks of boots and walking shoes both on the path and on the muddy earth at the edges. I walked more quickly down the hillside to the very bottom of the hill. There was an engraved metal sign fixed to a plate, proclaiming that the hill was owned by the National Trust and administered by Cadw. Near a gate set into the stone wall that marked both the boundary. At the gate to the lane outside the enclave there was a large information board in Welsh and English, giving the details and a brief history of the fort. I ignored both signs, pulled roughly at the gate and made my way unsteadily out onto the lane. Once there, I felt more secure. Ahead of me, down the lane, I could see the white painted walls of Clyffe House and I strode out eagerly.

After only a few minutes I reached the door to Clyffe House. The cottage was still in darkness; I assumed that the power was still off. Out of habit though as I walked into the hall, I reached for a light switch. The living room lights at once flared. The fire was still burning and had recently been built up.

"Sheila! Sheila!" I called. There was no reply. I left the living room and walked down one end of the long hallway. The doors to the kitchen and bathroom were both open, but neither room was occupied. Feeling alarmed, I walked down the other end of the corridor. I knocked on the first bedroom door, and called her name again. When there was no reply, I opened her bedroom door. The room was empty; the bed bare as the duvet was still in the living room. Cautiously I tried my bedroom door; this time the latch moved without fuss and I was able to open the door. The room was empty. Very cautiously I tried the door of the intervening bedroom, from which I had fallen into that awful tunnel below the house. I turned on the light, but that, too, was empty. I closed the door and looked back down the length of the corridor in consternation. Sheila was not here. I peered through the window in the wall that looked out into the yard. Sheila's car was still there; but I was alone in Clyffe House. Then I heard a rustling and a scratching noise from the living room, and the blood went cold in my veins.

Sheila raised the poker and looked around the end bedroom of Clyffe House. It was clear that the room was unoccupied and that Mister Jones had not tried to take his duvet from the bed. She stepped backwards into the hallway and closed the door. To her right was the unused bedroom, with her room beyond that. Surely, she thought, Mister Jones would not be in her bedroom? Tentatively she reached out and tried the latch. To her relief it moved, and she opened the door and looked inside. It was dark; nervously she raised the poker and swung it around in front of her. What light did come into the room through the window gave no illumination; but there was enough light for her to see that Mister Jones was not there. Nor, to her relief, was anyone or anything else. Sheila was not tempted to try and walk into that bedroom. Instead she closed the door firmly and then with some trepidation walked the few steps to the door of her own bedroom.

"I don't know if I want him to be in there or not," she said aloud. "In fact, I'm not sure which is the scariest idea." Voicing her fear aloud did not make it any easier, and realising that unless she acted now she might be too frightened to find out, Sheila pushed her own bedroom door open. There was no duvet on her bed, because of course, she realised, it was in the living room. But there was no Mister Jones either. Sheila lowered the poker and tried to decide if she was disappointed or not. "On the whole, I'm relieved," she said aloud again. Her voice was only a small sound in the quiet cottage, but she found that better than no sound.

"So, what now?" she asked herself. "Talking to myself? Isn't that the first sign of madness?" she giggled, and then stopped abruptly as even to herself she sounded a little hysterical. "So, where could Mister Jones have gone?" She closed her bedroom door, and contemplated the long hallway. "He came thisaway… but didn't go thataway, or he would have passed the living room and I would have seen him. No windows open… I wonder though if he could have gone outside? He isn't in the house, so he must have got out somehow."

Pleased with her logic, Sheila turned to one of the windows in the corridor that opened out onto the yard. She looked outside. Dimly she could see the shape of her Peugeot near the gate, but nothing else. Wait! There, outside in the lane, were people. She swung back away from the window, then shook her head at her own silliness. Clyffe Cottage was in darkness; no one could see her at the window. She looked out again. A small group, swinging electric torches to light their way, were walking past the entrance to the yard. It was very late, who could they be? Sheila wondered if they had come across Mister Jones, who clearly now was not inside Clyffe House. On an impulse, she decided to ask them. Running back down the corridor into the living room, she paused only to drop two more chopped logs onto the fire, before putting on her shoes. Leaving the front door ajar, she rushed out into the night to follow the small group down the lane.

At the gate, she looked left and right down the lane. To the left, only the shape of Caercaddug loomed against the night sky. To her right, the small group had reached the gate of Fferm Ffynnon. To her surprise, they opened the gate and went into the yard of the old farmhouse.

"What are they doing there?" Sheila said to herself, confused. She had seen how little there was at the old farm, and there was nothing she was sure to attract a group of walkers, if that was what they were. Suddenly, she was nervous about following them and looked back at Clyffe House. The front door was now firmly shut, although she was sure that she had left it open. "Between the devil and the deep blue sea," she muttered. "In for a penny, in for a pound," she added, and smiled at herself for using those ancient clichés, reassuring as they strangely were.

Sheila set off down the lane. The people ahead of her had now entered the yard of Fferm Ffynnon. None had looked back to see her, and she had felt reticent about calling out. The lane was uneven and she walked rather than ran, to avoid turning an ankle. The gate into Fferm Ffynnon had been closed and at first she struggled with the sliding latch. No one was now in sight, and Sheila swore under her breath. The gate dropped on its elderly hinges, and she struggled to open it enough to squeeze through the gap between the metal gate and the brick gatepost. At last, with a loud noise, the gate moved enough for her to get through.

The noise had sounded awfully loud and Sheila looked nervously around the deserted old farmyard. Part of her wanted to see the people she had followed, but at the same time she suddenly felt a bit nervous. It was very late at night for a group to be entering the grounds of a deserted farm, after all. But as the alternative was to go back to the dark cottage where her friend had just vanished, she decided that looking for company was a better option.

"Is anybody there?" she called out with sudden decision. "Hello? Help?" she added, hopefully. There was no reply. "Help!" she shouted, more loudly. Disturbed by her voice a dark bird flew low across the yard towards the trees on the far side of the yard, and she was startled. Sheila looked over her shoulder at the lane, but could see no one. She screwed up her courage and walked into the yard. To her right the broken windows of Fferm Ffynnon rose against the night. To her left she could dimly make out the shapes of the old farm's outbuildings. Vaguely she recalled that they had not seemed to be in poor condition, but Mr Davis had warned against them. Why? She could not remember. Perhaps those other people had gone into one of them, she thought. Sheila walked towards the nearest building. The windows were all covered with plywood sheeting, but in the corner where two buildings met was a door. She decided at least to try the door. Standing in front of it, she could see that like the rest of the outbuildings the door looked old and abandoned but had been used recently. The padlock was hanging open on a hasp and the door itself had not properly closed - perhaps it had warped, she wondered. Anyway, it was no longer locked, so Sheila took hold of the handle and pulled. To her surprise, the door swung open smoothly and silently.

"Now what?" she asked herself. The outbuilding was black inside, and she could see nothing. Still she stepped inside. The door swung shut behind her, and the impact closed it properly. Immediately the lights inside the outbuilding came on, and she gasped. Sheila had expected to see little more than an old and disused chicken shed. Instead the inside of the building was clean and well maintained. The floor was clean and clearly recently re-concreted. Sheila looked around in astonishment. The inside of the building was arranged in two wings set at right angles, but both were empty. Sheila walked down one wing to the very end. There were bolts and fastenings on the edges of the end wall. Sheila ran her hand over the wall, and it moved slightly. "Is this whole wall a door?" she wondered. Turning around she walked down to the junction with the other side of the building. She turned the corner and stopped short. This part of the mysterious and brightly lit outbuilding was devoid of furniture but did hold a substantial lift, and a well-lit and well-used set of stairs leading down, presumably into a basement below the building. It also held four people who were staring at her.

"Oh," Sheila said, surprised.

"Ah," said the nearest person to her. "Miss Balsam."

Sheila looked at him. "Mr Davis. Er, I suppose you are wondering what I'm doing here?" Recognising the owner of Clyffe House, she relaxed. Surely now she would be safe, and have some help in finding Mister Jones.

"Well, yes, I was rather, see." Mr Davis gave no sign of surprise, or of command, but his three companions walked deliberately around Sheila so that she was surrounded and her retreat to the way out was blocked.

"Actually, I was hoping to find you. Well, find anyone, really," said Sheila.

"Really? And why would you be doing that?"

"Well, my friend, Mister Jones…"

"Ah yes, I remember him."

"He seems to have vanished. I was wondering if you'd seen him at all while you've been walking about?"

The silent group exchanged glances and moved a little closer to Sheila. She looked at their faces , two women and a man; they all carried the same facial pockmarks and scars as Mr Davis, and she began to wonder just what was happening here, in this building disguised so well as a ruin.

"There's been a few funny things gone on you see at Clyffe House. Scary things. I think it's haunted, Mr Davis."

"You think Clyffe House is haunted?" Mr Davis just sounded curious. "Why ever would you be thinking that, then?"

"Well, the lights keep going on and off. The doors stick and then open mysteriously, and things, well…"

"Go bump in the night? So what happened to your friend, then?"

"I don't know," confessed Sheila. One of the women moved much closer to Sheila and examined her with curiosity. Sheila suddenly felt as if a predator was evaluating her and her fear returned. "He just vanished while inside the house."

"Are you sure he didn't just go for a walk outside?" asked Mr Davis. "Although that itself can be risky round here at night."

"Risky? Why?" asked Sheila.

"Never know who you might meet," smiled the woman nearest to her. "Lots of ghosts round here, see. It's an old land, and things... linger."

"Megan," said Mr Davis in a flat tone, frowning at her. "Be quiet." He turned back to Sheila. "Now, Miss Balsam, the question is, what are we going to do with you?"

Sheila stepped backwards against the wall. "I hoped you might help me, and help me find Mister Jones." She looked around the bare room and at the four people who she feared had just become her captors. "Though I expect as you said, he just popped out and will now be urgently looking for me!"

Mr Davis took another step towards her and Sheila shrank back against the wall, wondering what she had got herself into. Mr Davis nodded at Megan. Smiling, the woman reached for Sheila.

"Don't touch me..." warned Sheila. She tried to step backwards but the other woman was behind her, and shoved her towards Megan.

"Why, might we catch something?" chuckled Mr Davis. For some reason, all four found that joke hilarious. Sheila took advantage of the moment by trying to run past Megan. But the woman grappled her, and as Sheila struggled to break free the others closed in and seized her arms.

"Miss Balsam, you really should not have come trespassing," sighed Mr Davis. "Now you have given us a problem."

"She can go to…" started the other woman.

Mr Davis interrupted her. "Not now, Rhian. Not now."

"Iuan, we have a room downstairs," suggested the other man present.

"Morgan, so we do." Mr Davis looked at Sheila and thought for a moment. "Miss Balsam I am sorry, but you cannot be allowed to leave here."

"What are you going to do with me then?" Sheila looked around. She could see neither mercy nor pity in the eyes of her captors. "Are you going to… to hurt me?"

"We are assuredly not going to kill you, Miss Balsam."

Sheila relaxed and slumped a little in the captors' arms; but her captors did not relax their grip on her even though they were now taking her weight.

"But what we are going to do, well you will have to wait and see, won't you?"

Sheila was not reassured by that, although her immediate fears were put to one side.

"Morgan, Megan." Mr Davis had not raised his voice, yet his authority was absolute and those addressed looked attentively at him for their instructions.

Sheila had been hoping for this chance, and pushing Megan against the wall she pulled free from the hands holding her arms and ran. She was only a few paces from the door to the outside, to freedom, and with a cry of relief she pushed at the door. It flew back. Sheila stopped in her tracks. Then she took three rapid paces backwards. Her face, already pale in the lighting, became chalk white and she raised both hands in front of her as if to push away the nightmare vision confronting her. She tried to scream but no sound came out of her open mouth. Again she stepped backwards, away from the door. Slowly, not needing to lower its head to pass the low lintel, the Addanc walked into the outbuilding followed by two men who bore the same facial scars and marks as the others.

The Addanc looked imperiously around the room, then pointed at Sheila. "Explain," it demanded.

"Lord, we have an intruder," said Mr Davis. "We were about to confine her."

"You were? By letting her open the door to the outside?" The Addanc's voice was cold. Sheila looked at Mr Davis, and decided that he was probably as frightened as she was.

"Lord, I knew that Idris and Emlyn, these two behind you," Mr Davis waved at the two men standing behind the Addanc, "were outside and that she could not escape us."

The Addanc nodded, the crest on its head sending distorted shadows across the floor. "Very well, I will accept that."

Sheila decided that Mr Davis was really quite relieved, although he said nothing in reply.

"What will you do with her now?" The Addanc stepped closer to Sheila, and reached out with one forefinger. The nail on the end was quite clean, but smelt strongly of seawater and Sheila shuddered. The Addanc noticed, and laughed softly. It ran the fingernail down Sheila's face, and she shook. "A disgusting face," the Addanc said softly. "So horribly smooth. We shall have to deal with that. Oh yes, we will have to deal with that."

"What do you mean?" asked Sheila. Her voice betrayed her fear.

The Addanc ignored her and turned its reptilian head to look at Mr Davis. "What did you plan for her?" it asked, curiously.

"Lord, we planned to confine her in one of the basement rooms."

The Addanc nodded. "That will do very well for now." It waved dismissively at Sheila and Idris and Emlyn walked past it to take her by the arms. She made no resistance as they pulled her away from the Addanc, but when she realised that they intended to take her down the stairs into the basement, she started to struggle.

"Miss Balsam," Mr Davis said to her without taking his eyes away from the Addanc. "Please do not struggle like that. It is not our intention to cause you pain. Please cooperate with my friends."

Sheila looked over her shoulder at the motionless Addanc. She thought that its eyes gleamed malevolently as it looked at her, and she did not want to be confined in the building while it was there, or to which it might - later- have access. "You can't lock me up!" she protested. She couldn't take her eyes away from the creature with the reptilian head and the short, misshapen but human body.

"Well, in fact we can. Let's just be clear about this shall we? No one knows you are here. It's going to be a long time before anyone comes looking for you, and if they do, no one is going to search this place. Now please behave yourself." Mr Davis pointed at the stairs and jerked his head. Sheila's captors acknowledged the unspoken order and pulled at her arms. Sheila struggled again, but Idris and Emlyn were strong enough to hold her without difficulty. They forced her towards the stairs and Sheila was forced down them into the basement below the outbuilding. At the bottom of the short flight of steps was a corridor that was as brightly lit as the room above. Several doors opened from it, and at one end was the lift.

"Where?" Emlyn asked Idris.

"At the end. There's an empty store room."

They let go of Sheila, and as she started to turn to fight, Emlyn pushed her quite hard. She staggered and had to step backwards to keep her balance. Emlyn smiled nastily and pushed her again.

"That's enough," Idris said to him. He looked at Sheila. "No one is planning to hurt you, miss. If you just do as we ask, you will be fine, and I'll let you have this bottle of water."

Sheila looked at the bottle of spring water Idris held in his hand and realised how very thirsty she felt. She nodded and took another two paces backwards towards the door at the end of the corridor. Idris smiled encouragingly and he and Emlyn kept moving forwards towards her.

"Yes, okay," Sheila said. She dropped her head, and stepped backwards again. Then when Idris took a pace forward, she lunged for the space between the two men as hard as she could. Taken by surprise, Idris was pushed to one side. Emlyn, however, had been expecting something to happen. He stuck out one long leg and Sheila tripped over his foot and lost her balance. Emlyn seized her arm as she fell and swung her around. He almost threw her through the half-open door to the end storeroom and then slammed the door shut. Sheila was left inside the room in darkness. Hammering desperately on the door from the inside, she discovered that there was no handle on the inside of the door at all. Although it was not locked, she was shut inside in the darkness - and without the promised bottle of water.

Standing in the darkness at the window of Clyffe House, I again heard that strange scratching sound from the living room. The scratching stopped and was followed by a tinkling noise, as though something metallic, but light in weight, had been thrown across the room. Then an object that glittered in the faint glow from the fire that extended out into the corridor was flung out of the living room. It hit the front door and bounced back, rolling towards me until it came to a halt almost at my feet. When it stopped I just stood and stared at it for a long moment, unwilling at first to investigate. Eventually, I bent down and picked it up. It felt astonishingly cold, so cold that I thought my fingers would freeze to the surface as I held it up and examined it. It was the metal end of a tube of lipstick. I held it up in front of my face, and could just see that there was no lipstick left. It had been entirely used up.

Confused, I walked nervously to the entrance into the living room and peered cautiously around the corner. At first, I could see nothing, for the firelight was dim and fading as the fire burnt itself down. Certainly the room was empty and at first glance undisturbed. There on the coffee table lay Sheila's laptop, with our coffee cups close beside it. Her papers too were still in fairly neat piles and her duvet was heaped, rather than hurled, at one end of the couch she had been using earlier in the night. Again there was a slight, metallic sound inside the room. A second tube of lipstick rolled across the room and stopped at my feet. This too was clearly completely used up. Scattering sparks across the hearth, one of the smouldering logs in the fireplace shifted. Fire blossomed briefly, and the light of the flames rose. I stared around me in wonder and shock, for on every wall of the room, in Sheila's lipsticks, were the words **HELP ME HELP ME HELP ME** repeated over and over again.

I sat down on the end of the nearest couch and just looked at the walls. The message was not exactly cryptic, and even I could understand it, but I could not understand who was sending the message, or what sort of help they could want, what sort of help they wanted me to give them. The firelight dimmed again.

"What do you want?" I shouted on impulse. "Who are you?"

The logs shifted again in the fire and the flames rose up. The words scrawled across each of the three walls shone brightly in the flickering light. One of the bedroom doors slammed closed; the noise echoed in the hallway. Very unwillingly I stood up and looked out into the corridor. To my left, down to the kitchen and bathroom, the hall was empty. But to my right, at the very end of the corridor, stood the figure of a girl. Not Sheila: this girl was tall, very slender and with long hair. She wore a thin white dress, and as I watched she beckoned to me and walked into my bedroom. The door half closed behind her. A gust of intensely cold air swept over me and I shivered. The invitation was clear, but I had no intention of accepting her offer. I retreated back into the living room and sat down again. The bedroom door slammed shut again.

I turned and put some more wood on the fire. "There's no way I'm going anywhere but this room tonight!" I said forcefully and aloud, hoping that whoever or whatever was in this house with me would hear me and take the hint. The firelight died under the new wood and I started to panic, but then the flames licked up and around the new wood. The dry timber caught, the light in the hearth grew stronger, and I relaxed. I sat for some time - how long I do not know - before the fire, waiting for the next terrifying thing to happen to me. Time passed so slowly in that room with the horrifying message written in lipstick across all the walls. Twice more I made up the fire and then retired to the couch. I spread Sheila's duvet around me, more for the comfort than for the warmth, as the fire was burning strongly. At last, despite my desire to stay awake, drowsiness overcame me and I slumped down on the couch.

I was frightened by the appearance of what I assumed was the ghost inhabiting the house, frightened by - and for - my missing friend and frightened by the words written all across the walls. So frightened that in truth the fear had paralysed my ability to think or take action. I could do nothing, I reasoned, except wait for the dawn and pray that Sheila had returned by then from wherever she had gone. That she might not be able to do so, or that she might be desperately awaiting my help, was a horrible thought yet no plan of action presented itself to me. More than slightly ashamed of myself for not taking some action, I drifted into a fitful sleep.

At length the thin daylight filtering through the deeply inset windows roused me. I sat up with a start and fumbled for the duvet. It was missing. I looked around the living room - there was no sign of the duvet. With another start I realised that I was naked. Frantically I looked around the room; there were my clothes, stacked neatly on the other couch. I threw myself across the coffee table and grabbed at them. As I did so I realised that during the night the clothes had been taken from me as I slept, then thoroughly cleaned of all the traces of mud and dirt that had accumulated during my rough descent down the hillside. I stared at them in wonder; then hurriedly pulled on my underwear and trousers. Was this a sign that Sheila had come back while I was asleep and chosen not to disturb me? Her duvet was gone, and I felt more cheerful, if somewhat cold and embarrassed.

Feeling better too for being dressed I resolved to make some tea and have breakfast. After going to the kitchen and switching on the kettle, I realised that I had to make a decision about my missing friend; if she was indeed still missing, for surely no ghost would have treated my clothes so kindly last night. I walked down the corridor, and looked into each bedroom. To my surprise all three doors opened easily for me and each room was immaculate and empty. Sheila's duvet had been returned neatly to her bed overnight, but of Sheila herself there was still no sign, and I realised that as she was therefore still missing, I would have to take some action. But what?

Suddenly filled with a very unaccustomed resolution, I decided to go outside and have a look around. What I might achieve by that, I had no idea; but at least I would be doing something. Without bothering about socks, I pulled on some shoes and walked outside. I felt this effort had been rewarded at once as

Mr Davis was peering over the gate into the yard at Sheila's car.

"Bore da!" I called out, and Mr Davis acknowledged the morning greeting in Welsh with a smile and a wave. I walked over to join him at the gate.

"Bit of damage you've done there!" Mr Davis remarked, waving at the back of Sheila's Peugeot.

"Not me, Mr Davis. I wasn't driving."

He laughed. "Women drivers, eh? Neither of you got hurt, though, I hope?"

"No, just a minor thing."

"Are you both enjoying your break here, then?" he asked me.

"Well, yes and no. We have had a few queer things happen in the cottage. And my friend went out last night but hasn't got back yet and I'm really rather worried about her."

Mr Davis gave me a keen look. "You and her, you are...?" he stopped, apparently unsure how to put the obvious question.

"We're just friends. Neighbours back home, but just friends."

"Right. Well then, maybe she met someone and, well, decided to stay over?"

I thought about that. While most unlike Sheila, I had to admit that it was not impossible. "I was more worried that she might have gone walking and had an accident, to be honest."

"Aye, well, the paths round here can be a bit slippery. But my dog and I are out and about all morning, we'll keep an eye out.

You mark my words though, she'll just have met some lad and forgot about everything else! Good morning to you!" Mr Davis nodded genially, whistled to his collie dog who was happily nosing about in some long grass on the verge, and walked off.

That had given me something to think about. His suggestion would have been quite out of character for Sheila Balsam, but it wasn't exactly impossible. And I suspected that the local police, if approached, would take the same view. Sheila had been away from the house overnight. That was all. The fact that I suspected something unexpected and unwelcome had befallen her would be ignored; at least for some time.

I walked slowly back into Clyffe House. I stood at the entrance to the living room and stared at the message that had been scrawled over and over and over again across the walls; and wondered just who exactly had written it, and what exactly I ought to do now.

Chapter five

Sheila blinked and threw her arm across her eyes at the blinding glare of the sudden bright light. She was sitting down with her back against a wall of the underground storeroom; both frightened and very, very uncomfortable. The burst of light that came through the open door from the underground corridor stopped her from attempting to escape. Iuan Davis had been tense, waiting and ready for her to run at him in an effort to break free from the storeroom, and so he relaxed when she stayed on the floor.

"I've brought you some food and water," he told her, turning on the light in the storeroom as well.

Shielding her eyes with one arm, Sheila glared at him. "How long are you keeping me here?"

Mr Davis stepped forward and carefully put the bottle of water and the packet of sandwiches out of Sheila's reach; then he stepped backwards to the door.

Sheila opened her eyes fully as she adjusted to the light. She looked at the food and water, and then looked at the door that was blocked by Mr Davis. "How long?" she asked again.

Mr Davis shrugged. "Miss Balsam, we do not normally have visitors here. Or unexpected guests. I cannot tell you because I do not know."

"Visitors? You mean prisoners!"

"I mean anyone. It's not our habit to lock people up, you see."

"What do you do with them, then?" asked Sheila.

"Do you really want to know, Miss Balsam? If you do, I can ask Emlyn to come and tell you. He enjoys that sort of thing, and he'll make sure you get all the information. Every last detail, if you follow me."

"Well, perhaps not then," Sheila replied in a small voice. "That thing. That monster. What is it?"

"He, Miss Balsam, he. Not thing. Not monster. Not it. *He*. He has lived here much, much longer than you can even imagine."

"I can well believe it!" Sheila picked up the bottle of water and took a long drink.

Mr Davis watched her drink and shook his head. "You may wish to ration yourself a little, Miss Balsam."

"Why?"

Mr Davis gave her an apologetic smile. "As you can see, we have no toilet facilities in this storeroom. And until I am instructed otherwise, this is where you are staying."

Sheila coloured. "You mean I have to…"

"Sorry." Mr Davis didn't really sound apologetic now. He stepped outside the room and closed the door. She heard the sound of the door locking.

"At least leave the light on!" yelled Sheila: but either Mr Davis did not hear her, or he took no notice. The storeroom light went out and Sheila was plunged back into darkness. She slumped back down against the wall, and sat awkwardly on the floor. She breathed in and out heavily, as deeply as she could. Then she made a conscious effort to take some control of herself - if she failed, she thought, the next step on the downward spiral was hysteria, and that was not an appealing prospect. "I'm worth more than that!" she said aloud in a fierce tone. "I'm better than that!" Again she breathed in and out, controlling her breathing as much as she could. Being alone in a dark place was an old childhood terror or nightmare of hers, and those long-banished fears rushed to return now. She shivered and wrapped her arms around herself.

Feeling a little better, Sheila searched her memory. She was sure that she remembered a lecture, or a TV programme, or maybe a radio piece or a newspaper article, on how to cope with being confined. There was a reality TV thing she thought, where the contestants were buried alive and have to last out as long as possible. This was just the same, she thought, although this room was bigger. What were the contestants taught or told to do? Because that would work for her. She tore the wrapping off the sandwich and ate the first half. Then, thinking that it might be some time before Mr Davis came back again, she laid the other half of the sandwich to one side. She thought about the water, but remembering that the room had no toilet facilities, decided to leave it a little longer before drinking.

The darkness of the room began to feel oppressive again and Sheila repeated her deep breathing exercise. "I will not panic. I will not panic. I am strong. I am strong. I am better than this; I am better than this," she repeated to herself over and over again like a mantra. "I am strong. I am strong," she said to help convince herself.

"I am glad to hear it," a cold voice replied.

Sheila became still and quiet immediately.

"I seek only the strong."

Sheila strained her eyes to peer through the darkness to see the speaker. "Who are you?" she asked. "Where are you?"

"I forgot, you cannot see in this level of light, can you?"

"No. No, I can't. It's too dark!"

There was a chuckle. Sheila thought, in the circumstances, it was quite a sinister sound and she made sure that her back was against the wall of the storeroom. She felt the air move softly against her cheek, and wondered if the door to the storeroom had been opened? She tensed and turned in the direction she hoped that she remembered led to the door before bracing her leg against the wall. The chuckle came again. But this time, rather than being cold, Sheila thought that it had a thin and predatory note. She pushed hard with her back foot and leapt as hard as she could. However, she only hit a solid wall, not an open door. She felt wildly around with both hands but could not feel either hinges or a handle. The chuckle came again.

"Missed," said the voice, amused.

"You don't know what I was aiming at!" replied Sheila. Now that the initial surprise had worn off she was in a state of real fear. Locked in a dark room with an unknown person was one of her nightmares. She had read many of the legends of the Minotaur; was that what was locked in here with her? A dreadful monster from ancient times? She threw her arms out wide and spun around. But her right wrist cannoned painfully into some metal storage racking and she cried out in pain. The racking shook and nearly overbalanced; at the far end of the storeroom something unidentified fell from the shelving and shattered on the concrete floor.

"Whoops. Please be more careful. Not everything in this room is safe - or indeed unbreakable."

"Don't!" shouted Sheila, rubbing her wrist. "Why are you doing this?"

"A good question," replied the unseen tormentor. "In fact, several very good questions, all wrapped together. I do wonder which one you might mean? Which one I should answer?"

"Where are you?"

"I am here and now."

"Very mystical," retorted Sheila. The overwhelming fear that she had felt at first hearing the voice in the lonely darkness was reducing now to a level that allowed her to think and not just react to the terror.

"Yes."

"Well, who are you, then?"

"I am the one talking to you from the darkness
I am he that stands apart
The darkness within the shadow at the edge of your sight
The sudden hand on your shoulder
The warm breath on your neck
The waking dream that visits you when you sleep
I am all that you need

And when your hand reaches out
You will find me waiting."

The side of Sheila's neck suddenly went cold. Sheila reached up and tentatively touched her skin. She felt nothing and was unsure if she was relieved, or disappointed. She stretched out her hand but again felt nothing except some cold metal shelving racks. "Doesn't tell me much," she grumbled.

"It tells you all you need to know."

"I reached out my hand."

"And here I am, waiting..."

Sheila still felt afraid. "The darkness is not my friend."

"Light, then. You would like some light?"

"I'm locked in here. Mr Davis turned the light off. But surely you are locked in here too? Whoever you are."

Sheila heard a hissing, sibilant laugh. "I'm in here with you, don't forget. And while you may be imprisoned in here, I am assuredly not. At least, not in the way you imagine."

"What other way is there?"

"Sheila..."

"How do you know my name?" demanded Sheila.

"I know many things. But in this case I was told by Iuan Davis."

"So you aren't a prisoner like me. You are one of them." Sheila's fear for herself, which had been abating during the conversation, returned.

"Not so. Perhaps the other way around."

"Why don't you turn the light on then?"

"Not yet, Sheila. In a little while, perhaps. I'm enjoying the chance to talk with you."

"What difference will the light make? I like to see who I'm talking to."

"Have you not yet guessed who that is?"

"Guessing games? No. I haven't. I know that you aren't Mr Davis, so I thought you were one of his friends, sent here to torment me, to frighten me."

"And are you afraid?"

"What do you think?" asked Sheila. "I've been dragged down here and locked up in the dark. Then, when I think I'm alone, you start talking to me from the other side of the room and won't turn the light on!" Even to herself, the last remark sounded a little petulant, and Sheila suddenly wished that she could unsay it.

"What are you afraid of, Sheila? Death?"

"Of course I am! Isn't everyone afraid of dying?"

"There are many ways to die. Sometimes, you can die a little inside and become something else, a change rather than an ending. Not all death is an end. But some ends are worse than death."

Sheila did not find that a reassurance and said so.

"What would you say, then, if I offered you a way to live?"

"To live? You were thinking of... killing me, then?" Sheila tried to keep the fear from her voice, but failed.

Again she heard that cold chuckle. "You misunderstand me. I was offering you a chance to live. Not forever, maybe, but certainly for a very long time." Sheila heard a long sigh, suddenly filled with a sadness that almost broke her heart. "I have been alone, and very lonely, for a very, very long time, Sheila. Do you know what loneliness can do to someone? How it can affect them?"

"I'm on my own. I live on my own. But I've got friends, so I'm not lonely," Sheila said firmly.

"Perhaps. But when you wake in the night, do you never wish for the comfort of a touch? Of companionship?"

"No. I'm not that sort of girl."

The cold laugh filled the storeroom, then was followed by a different, softer sound. With a start of surprise, Sheila realised she was hearing the sound of soft crying. "How long have you been alone, then?" she asked.

"Too long, Sheila, too long. It has been many years now. I dislike having no companionship. But those who have offered me companionship down the many years have, well, not been what I might have hoped. In you, I see something a little different, something a little special."

Despite herself, Sheila was flattered. She could not recall being called special. In the recent years, she had lived with her cantankerous, domineering and dismissive mother whose recent death had freed her from a life of near slavery to the older woman's demands. She had been called many things in those recent years, but few of them were pleasant. This was a new experience for her. Mister Jones' gentle courtesy towards her was nice, but of a different order to this conversation.

"Who are you, and why are we still in the dark?" she asked.

"I'll turn on the light in just a little while, just for you."

"Well, tell me your name, then."

"My name? In truth, it is so long since I used it, since I needed to use it, that I have almost forgotten it."

"Everyone has a name. You know mine, so if you want to carry on chatting me up in this way, you can at least tell me who you are!"

"My people have long been gone, leaving me alone, as I said; and so I have had no need now of a personal name. Down the long years since I have lived in this region of Prydain, I have been known as Addanc."

Sheila gasped, her hand flying to her mouth.

"Come," said the Addanc with a hint of both entreaty and bitterness in his tone, "live with me and be my love."

The Addanc turned on the light in the storeroom, and walked out from behind one of the storage racks. Sheila looked fully on the Addanc as he held out one hand to her. She screamed, and fainted, falling heavily to the floor. The Addanc turned out the light in the room and in the darkness he moved towards the unconscious girl.

*

I went into the kitchen of Clyffe House and made some tea. I do seem to drink a ridiculous quantity of tea, and especially in any sort of crisis. But, I had to ask myself as I carried the mug of tea back into the living room and sat down by the now cold fire, was this a crisis? Last night, in the darkness and with the frighteningly intense supernatural activity taking place all around me, I had no doubt that Sheila's disappearance was a crisis. But in the cold light of day, especially after listening to Mr Davis's suggestion, I was less sure. Could Sheila simply have met some young man and, well, spent the night with him? Briefly, I felt a flicker of envy. No, to be honest, perhaps of jealousy. Sheila was my neighbour, my friend, and nothing more lay between us. Yet occasionally late at night, I had thought that a little more might become possible. I had always shrugged off the idea as arising from the occasional weakness or loneliness for although I am very comfortable with my solitary life, who has not at some time thought of a companion? Who has not needed a companion when the dark of the night seems to last forever and the hands of the clock crawl so slowly towards the hour of the dawn?

Still, it remained that Sheila and I were only friends, and my friend had gone out into the night and not returned. She had not taken her bag and in my admittedly limited experience of women that was most unusual. As, of course, was the writing on the wall in her lipstick. I drank my tea and thought. The most important issue was Sheila's disappearance. Assuming that she was unable to return to Clyffe House of her own accord, then two possibilities came to mind; either she had met with some accident, and was perhaps injured nearby waiting for me to rescue her or she was unable to return because someone was preventing her. The second problem was the supernatural activity. Could the two be linked? Had Sheila been seized by a ghost, or something worse? I knew of a number of things of that nature that would gladly take hold of a young woman for a variety of reasons. I also knew of a man whose pleasure, delight and purpose was thwarting such things. Would - or could - my friend Eric be able to help?

I knew what his first question would be. Had I taken the most obvious and simple approach - that of walking around the property to see if I could find my friend, hurt and unable to walk? That had to be my first task; to go and walk around the house and the immediate surroundings and see if Sheila was in difficulties. If I could not find her, then I could rule out that possibility and think about acting accordingly.

Although I prefer action to inaction, making difficult choices or acting decisively does not come naturally or easily to me, so I was relieved to have made a decision on which I could act. Putting down my mug of tea half finished I left the living room and walked out into the yard, carefully closing the front door behind me. First, I decided, I should walk around the house and also check Sheila's car. The car was nearby, so I opened the door and peered inside. The car was empty; or at least, looking at the litter lying around for Sheila was not the tidiest of car users, it was innocent of any bodies. There was insufficient room in the boot for a body, so I closed the car door and looked around the yard. "That way!" I decided, and at random walked towards the side of the house that led to the Coastal Path. Standing at the corner of the house I shaded my eyes and searched the fields ahead, but could see nothing. There were no ditches or hedges that might conceal her if she were lying there.

I walked along the back wall of the house, but aside from the rubbish bins there was little to be seen. My hopes of finding her close by now rested on the last side of the property. I breathed heavily as I rounded the last corner of the building, praying inwardly that she would be there. The remaining side of the property was left to rough ground and overgrown, but there was no sign of Sheila. I let out the breath I had not realised that I was holding.

Walking back to the yard, I went out through the gate and into the lane. Which way? I looked at Caercaddug with some foreboding. But that seemed the most likely possibility for Sheila to have got herself hurt and been unable to get back to the cottage, so I set off down the lane to the ancient hill fort. Passing through the gate from the lane I walked slowly up the sloping path towards the top of the hill, calling Sheila's name intermittently. In the daylight, the deep ditches surrounding the hilltop seemed quite innocuous. It did not take me long to walk around the top of the site and it was clear that Sheila was not there. With a sigh I trudged back down the path until I reached the lane, and then paused for breath at the wall.

The last place to search would be Fferm Ffynnon. Feeling somewhat despondent, I set off along the lane, past Clyffe House, toward the ruined farmhouse. I never actually walked into the old farmyard, however. As I reached the rusting metal gate, Mr Davis appeared in the yard with his collie dog at his heels.

"Hello," he called out cheerfully.

"Mr Davis," I greeted him by name.

"Out for a walk is it, then?"

"I'm just looking for my friend. Miss Balsam. She's not home yet and I'm worried, as you know."

"Well, it's as I said, Mister Jones. I'll bet she's met a young man. I've been all over the land round here this morning, and not seen hide nor hair of her. Even been out to the cliffs, I have, but seen no trace of her."

"I'm not sure that I'm relieved," I told him.

"Never pleased, so you're not! Your friend isn't hurt in a ditch as far as I can tell, so that's all to the good, isn't it?"

"Yes, yes. Of course you're right, Mr Davis."

"Don't you be worried, now. She'll be home, just like a teenager stopping out late, you'll see." Mr Davis pulled hard at the gate and created a big enough gap for him to squeeze through. His collie followed obediently and Mr Davis pulled the gate firmly shut behind him and then leant on it. The inference was very clear. He clapped me on the top of my arm in a friendly fashion and nearly knocked me over. I tried to peer past him over the gate into the farmyard, but he blocked my view. I had no option but to accept his word, and so I walked disconsolately back towards Clyffe House. Halfway down the lane I looked back toward Fferm Ffynnon. Mr Davis was still standing at the gate of the ruined farm, watching me. He waved cheerfully. I raised my hand in acknowledgement and carried on walking.

At the entrance to Clyffe House, I stopped and looked around. My first option, and my best hope, had failed. Sheila was not lying hurt in a ditch or field near the house. I walked back into the yard and examined her car. I am not an expert, but the damage looked somewhat superficial and so I resolved that maybe I could drive the Peugeot. I can drive although I own no car; living in a city with good public transport has meant that I have had no need for a vehicle of my own. Where would the keys be? I recalled that Sheila had left her handbag so maybe the car keys were there, inside the cottage.

I left the car and walked into the cottage. I had two remaining options; either I could telephone the police and report Sheila missing with all that would entail, including being told that my friend had probably gone off with some man she had met; or I could assume that she had met with foul play and call for some reinforcements to assist me. After the inexplicable events at the cottage over the last few days I knew exactly who I should call on for help; my friend Eric. He had a wide experience of the supernatural and paranormal and I trusted him implicitly. But, as I did, he lived in the city and did not drive.

Clyffe House had no telephone, but I thought that I had seen Sheila's mobile phone in the cottage. With sudden determination I strode into the house; if Sheila had indeed left her mobile on the coffee table in the living room, then for me that would be all the evidence I required that she had not gone from the cottage voluntarily; for, unlike me, she belonged to a generation that could not bear to be parted from their phones. As soon as I walked through the door I could see her phone. The feeling that something dreadful had happened to her rolled over me like a crashing wave and I sat down on the couch. I picked up the phone and looked at it. Fortunately Sheila did not bother with a password and so I was able to see immediately that, although low, the mobile phone possessed enough usable battery to allow me to make a call or two.

I dialled a number that I knew off by heart and as I did so I looked with more attention at the living room wall. I almost dropped the phone in shock; where that wall had been covered with the same message as the other walls, using the same red lipstick, the wall above and around the hearth had changed: the message **HELP ME** had changed. Now the lipstick script read **HELP HER HELP HER HELP HER HELP HER.**

That was the final straw. With immediate resolution I dialled Eric's number and listened to the ring tone cycle and recycle. "Come on, Eric, come *on,*" I whispered aloud to myself. The relief I felt when the call was answered was overwhelming.

"Hello?"

"Hello, Eric!"

"Why, Mister Jones. Is this a pleasant surprise, or have you managed to get yourself into trouble- again?"

"Eric... I'm not in trouble. But someone else is. I need your help."

There was a sigh at the other end of the telephone. "You know exactly how to push my buttons, don't you Mister Jones? So, what has happened?"

"My neighbour and I, that's Sheila Balsam, you have met her before, came away for a bit of a break."

"Do I offer my congratulations?"

"It's not like that, Eric, and you know it! We are just friends, as I seem to have to keep telling everyone."

"Of course, Mister Jones, of course."

I made an exasperated noise into the telephone, and Eric chuckled. I continued my story. "Anyway, this cottage we took is haunted. We've had some very odd things happen. Then I ended up in a tunnel and had to escape and now Sheila has disappeared completely."

"How long has she been gone?" asked Eric, in a calm and neutral tone I presume he thought I would find reassuring.

"Since late on yesterday."

"Then either there is nothing to worry about, or fast action is needed. Why do you think you need my help? Rather than the police?"

"Eric, last night the walls of the living room were covered in writing, in her lipstick, saying 'Help me'.

"In Sheila's writing?" asked Eric.

"I really don't think so. But today, the words have changed to 'Help her' instead."

"Hum. It's all a bit, well, isn't it?"

"Eric, there's a lot of weird stuff gone on here. Too much to talk about on the phone, and I'm extremely worried about her. I think she's in trouble."

"Where are you?"

I described the location of Clyffe House, and Eric wrote down the address.

"Good heavens, Mister Jones, you really are in the back of beyond there. If I am to help you out, how do I get there?"

"Sheila's car is here. But it's been damaged, and I'm not insured to drive it."

"So, I need to make my own way, then. Mister Jones, I do so enjoy our conversations!"

"Eric, I'm sorry. But I do need your help. Look, there's no point in me calling the police. They'd just say that she hadn't been gone very long, and wait for a bit."

"That is sensible advice."

"But I do know Sheila. She'd never go off without her handbag containing her mobile phone and her lipstick! She just wouldn't."

Eric made a non-committal noise and I realised that he needed a little more convincing.

"The doors seem to lock and open at random," I told him. "The lights do strange things, and someone keeps trying to send spooky messages by writing on the walls."

"Spooky messages." Eric was clearly dismissive.

"I fell into a trap, and had to walk down a tunnel to a nearby ancient hill fort to escape."

"A secret tunnel. Well, well. A tourist attraction perhaps?"

"I did wake up when a skeleton climbed into my bed," I told him in an effort to engage him a little more.

"Really?" asked Eric. "Now that's actually interesting! Whose skeleton was it?"

"I didn't get a chance to ask. Eric, please. I'm really, really worried for my friend."

"Oh, very well then. I wouldn't mind a visit to that part of the coast anyway, and a day out will do me good."

"Eric," I said with relief, "I'm so grateful. Honestly, thank you."

"We'll talk more when I get there. I know that it isn't far, but there is no train service. I'll work something out."

Eric disconnected and I put Sheila's phone down with a satisfied sigh. At last, proper professional help was on its way. Then the hairs on the back of my neck rose, and a chill ran down my spine. The ancient warning of the human race; the warning that we are being closely observed by a predator, by one who means us harm, the warning that sparks the will to flight or fight. Looking at the floor of the living room I could tell by the changed light that the front door of Clyffe House had been opened wide, and shadows fell into the room and lay across my feet. The shadows shifted, and unwillingly I raised my head to see who, or what, was threatening me now. Three figures loomed in the doorway, blocking out the light. As I looked up, they moved closer.

Eric put down the handset thoughtfully. His telephone lay on a small table in his hall so he went back into his living room and sat down on a chair beside his fire. As was his custom a small wood fire was burning there, and he stared for few moments at the flames, thinking deeply. On the wall behind him hung a woven tapestry with an image of Vishnu; a small altar was set below the tapestry and a square of carpet lay before it. Eric stood, approached the tapestry and altar and bowed three times. Then he sat in a meditation pose on the square of carpet, and chanted part of an ancient prayer to Vishnu The Preserver.

Santhakaram Bujaga sayanam Padmanabham suresam

Viswadharam Gagana sadrusam Megha varnam shubangam

Lakshmi kantham kamala nayanam Yogi hrid dyana gamyam

Vande vishnum bava bhayaharam sava lokaika nadham

Eric closed his eyes and composed himself. Then he slipped easily into a comfortable meditative state. He repeated his personal mantra over and over again and felt a deep calm fill his senses. After some minutes, he bowed again while still seated. Then he rose and left the room. He climbed the stairs to his bedroom, found a small suitcase and filled it with some clothes. He pulled a sports bag from below his bed and carrying both the bag and the suitcase went back downstairs. Leaving the bags in the hall, he extinguished the small fire in the hearth. As the aromatic smoke filled the room Eric examined the books on his bookcase. Mister Jones had given him no information of use, just a plea for help. He was accustomed to being able to use his reference library when faced with a problem, and so looked at his collection of reference books pensively. "So, maybe it's time to show that I can be a 'Paranormal and Supernatural Consultant' who does not always need to consult his library," Eric said to himself.

He went to the altar and picked up a number of items. The altar comprised a small table with two drawers. From one drawer he took some bundles of herbs and from the other some small vials of water. Checking that the fire was properly out, he left his living room and closed the door. In the hall he added the herbs and water to the sports bag which already held the things he liked to consider his emergency kit. From a closet he took a jacket, shoes, and a thick overcoat, all of which he put on. Finally Eric went into his kitchen, checked that the back door was locked and that only the fridge was left switched on. As an afterthought, he quickly went back into the living room and selected three books from the library and the novel he was reading from a side table near the fire.

Returning to the hall, he slipped the books into the sports bag then picked up the bags and left his house. Before closing the front door behind him though, he put down the bags, bowed to the empty hall and muttered a long sentence. When the door was closed and locked he ran his open palms over the doorframe, paying particular attention to the handle, the lock and the hinges, again chanting quietly. These precautions taken, he lifted the two bags, wincing slightly at the weight of the suitcase, and left his property.

Around the corner from his house was a bus stop and the first bus along took him to the coach station in the city centre. Fortunately, the National Coach Company ran a service with a stop that was close to his destination and he bought a ticket. The coach would depart shortly too, which Eric found a relief; he had not been looking forward to spending time sitting idly in the waiting room. He didn't drink coffee and doubted that he would find the tea on offer in the café to his taste, so he had been spared that as well. When he was able to board the coach he quickly took a window seat about half way down and looked out with a feeling of excitement. He always enjoyed travelling for some distance, and had done since he had been a child. A coach journey of around three hours through some of the best scenery in West Wales would be a pleasant trip he decided, and the novel stayed in his sports bag. When it was time for the coach to leave, it was about half full of passengers.

The first part of the journey was unremarkable as the coach passed through the outskirts of the city and joined the motorway. Before too long though the driver left the busy motorway and turned onto smaller roads. Although still classed as main roads and carrying a lot of traffic, these roads twisted and turned, passing wild moorland, small villages and towns and many farms in various states of repair. Occasionally the coach stopped in some of the towns and villages, letting off some passengers and sometimes taking on more. Eric had never actually been in this particular part of Wales and he looked out avidly, drinking in the wild beauty and the noticing the contrast between some of the small towns and villages - some were clearly prosperous while others had fallen on hard times. But the weather was kind, the sky a vivid blue, and even the less well-kept houses held a charm for Eric's approving gaze.

At last, to Eric's disappointment, the coach came to a halt in the seaside town that was as close to his destination as it went. Eric thanked the driver as he left, and with a sense of regret watched the coach take onboard a few more passengers and then drive away. The town was full of Georgian era houses and shops, and the residents all looked happy and cheerful as they bustled around. Eric looked around and saw a taxi parked on the other side of the road. The driver was eating a sandwich, and drinking something from a flask. He looked mildly annoyed at being interrupted when Eric tapped on his window.

"Where do you want to go, then?" he asked, putting down the remains of his sandwich.

Eric passed him the slip of paper with Clyffe House's address on it. The taxi driver glanced at it, and then gave it a hard look. He passed the piece of paper back to Eric. "No," he said shortly. Then he wound up his window and drove off, leaving Eric on the pavement.

Eric looked after the departing taxi with interest. "That's curious," he said aloud. Behind him was a newsagent's shop with a large number of business cards in the window. He looked at the cards, and as expected there were several adverts from taxi firms. He took out his mobile and rang the first. The driver himself answered. When he gave the destination, the driver said curtly that he was too busy and disconnected. The next two taxi companies did the same and Eric was becoming very intrigued. Before he rang the fourth taxi, he took a map of the area out of his pocket and studied it. This time he gave the taxi driver a destination near to Clyffe House, rather than the cottage itself and the driver readily agreed. Eric waited patiently, thankful that it wasn't raining, and after five minutes the taxi arrived.

"You wanting Pont yr Aber?" called the driver through the window.

"That's me!" replied Eric cheerfully. He opened the back door of the taxi and pushed his bags across the seat before sliding in himself.

"You on holiday, then?" asked the driver, checking his mirrors and driving away.

"No, just visiting friends nearby."

"Right. Been round here before at all, have you?"

"No, first time. Lovely area."

"Yes, lots of tourists, we get," said the driver.

He lapsed into silence and turned off the main coast road onto narrow lanes, driving carefully. Eric looked out of the window, but the view was mainly of high hedges and little else could be seen. The car passed a signpost for Fferm Ffynnon and Clyffe House, and Eric noted them. "What's down there?" asked Eric.

"Nothing," replied the driver.

"My friends said there was a holiday cottage down there; I thought it might be worth my hiring it?"

"I wouldn't," said the driver. "Doesn't have a good reputation locally."

"Really?" asked Eric. "What's wrong with it then?"

"No one knows anyone who's ever enjoyed their time there. And the lane isn't well looked after, so none of the taxi drivers round here want to go down there."

"Right." Eric accepted the explanation at face value, but decided that the reaction of the other drivers had been too strong for that to be the only reason. He decided that he was becoming more interested in this place, and that Mister Jones might actually be in trouble. Mister Jones had never called him for help before without actually being in trouble, but other contacts had called for Eric's aid without actually needing his rather specialist help and he had become reserved about offering his assistance.

The taxi driver stopped amongst a small cluster of houses. "Right mate," he said. "Which one did you want?"

Eric looked at the small village. There was a small pub whose door was open. Eric made a show of looking at his watch. "My friends won't be back just yet. I'll grab a drink first, while I wait."

The taxi driver gave him an odd look, but said no more. Eric gave him some money, and when the driver started to look for some change, shook his head.

"Thanks, mate," said the driver.

Eric opened the door, pulled his bags out from the car, and wandered over to the door of the pub. The taxi driver made hard work of turning around and gave Eric a long look; but Eric was at the door of the pub and so he drove away. Eric waited a few minutes to give the driver time to depart, then set off walking back up the lane. Before long he came to the junction where the freshly painted sign announced the way to Clyffe House. He studied the surface of the track and decided that it was probably sufficiently rough to deter a taxi driver. Yet Mister Jones' friend had driven down the track to the cottage, for Mister Jones had said that he had access to a car. Perhaps the state of the surface was the reason for the damage?

Reserving judgement, Eric set off down the lane. He turned the corner and looked down the length of the track to help orientate the scene in the mind. On his left lay a ruined farmhouse, beyond it a gate and a sign for Clyffe House. At the far end of the track rose a hill, with a path climbing the face of the hill and deep ditches surrounding the top. Eric stopped walking and stared at the hill. Something about it spoke to him of dark times and dark deeds, and he felt uncomfortable. Could that be the real reason that the taxi drivers avoided this place? Still, Mister Jones was now only a short distance down the track at the clearly signed Clyffe House, so Eric set off again. Level with the gate into the yard of the ruined farmhouse, he staggered sideways and dropped his suitcase.

Breathing hard, Eric stared at the ruins of Fferm Ffynnon and the apparently neglected outbuildings. The sheer force of the malignancy he could feel from the farmyard had taken him by surprise, but he could see no immediate threat. Picking up his suitcase, he steeled his nerve and went on. Once he had passed by the gateway, the weight of the baleful miasma seemed to fade, and he walked more easily. At the gate to Clyffe House however, he stopped. It was important, he decided, to take a careful first impression of this place.

The gate into the yard was a double gate made of varnished wood opening to a width of around twelve feet. He could see a small Peugeot car parked inside the yard, with some damage visible on one corner. The rest of the yard was bounded by a stone wall. Clyffe House itself was a long single story building with several windows and tubs of bright flowers at intervals along the wall. The closed front door was of varnished wood, and the property looked cheerful and inviting, in contrast to the statement by the taxi driver that no one enjoyed staying there.

Eric put down his suitcase and reached out to the gate. When his hand touched the gate he froze. After a moment, he shook himself, and a single tear left his right eye and rolled down his cheek. "So much pain, so much hurt," he whispered. With an effort he pushed the gate open and strode into the yard, his suitcase forgotten. He looked around, expecting to see something after the shattering emotion he had felt through the gate, but there was nothing. Cautiously he approached the front door and using the sports bag rather than his hand, pushed at the door. Silently it swung open. Eric paused, half expecting another rush of emotion to pour over him. When that did not happen, he put one foot inside the hall.

The corridor felt cold. Eric looked around, but could see no one. Before him was the living room, but no Mister Jones. He shouted, and the echo of his voice returned to him from each end of the corridor, but that was his only reply. Eric stepped gingerly into the hallway, alert to any possible danger. He looked at the living room and the words scrawled across the walls with some astonishment.

"Well," he said aloud, "you wanted to make your message clear, didn't you?"

One of the fire irons fell over in the grate, and Eric looked at it thoughtfully. "Was that you, or one of you, I wonder?" He waited, but the house remained still and silent. The daylight was beginning to fail now, so Eric put his sports bag down deliberately on the coffee table. "Do not touch!" he ordered the empty room.

Going back outside, he shivered slightly when he looked out across the yard towards the ruins of Fferm Ffynnon. "That's bad, but is it the centre?" he mused. Shaking his head he went over to the gate and picked up his suitcase. He stepped outside the gate back onto the lane. Looking up and down the lane he could see a man with a dog watching him from the low wall that surrounded the hill. Eric waved, but the man did not acknowledge the gesture. Eric shrugged, closed the gate and returned inside Clyffe House. Now accepting the growing darkness, Eric turned on the lights and closed the front door. He looked along the corridor towards the three doors at the end. "A bedroom," he said aloud. "I need a bedroom." Obligingly, one of the three doors at the end of the hallway creaked open.

Eric looked suspiciously at the open doorway. "Really?" he said aloud. The door creaked invitingly. Cautiously Eric approached the door and pushed it further open. Inside, the room was dark, and he could see little. The furniture was merely a shadow, and the floor a sea of darkness. "Maybe not," he mused. He took a step backwards, then to one side. First he tried the latch of the door to his right. It would not move as though it was locked. Thoughtfully he put down his suitcase and tried the remaining door that was set in the end wall of the corridor. That handle too refused to open the door. The middle door opened wider, without his help.

"Don't think so!" Eric said firmly, and walked back to the living room. Behind him, the bedroom door slammed shut. Eric checked his pace but then continued. In the living room, his first move was to light the fire. The ashes of the last fire he swept neatly into a pile on the side of the hearth. Kneeling before the grate he laid the smaller kindling in a pyramid shape, then added some sheets from the unused pad of notepaper that Sheila had left lying on one of the couches, and using a box of matches from his pocket he set the wood alight. A sudden cold draft made the small flames flicker and falter but Eric quickly shielded the small fire with his hands and body; the flames grew back and gradually set the kindling alight. Eric nodded in satisfaction and added some larger pieces of wood. When the flames licked happily around those, Eric moved back from the hearth and got up.

It was time, he decided, to examine the rest of the house. Leaving the living room he deliberately did not look to his right towards the bedrooms but concentrated on the other direction of the hall. There were two doors to his left, identical in size and colour to the bedroom doors at the other end of the corridor. He opened the first and looked around the kitchen. There were two used mugs on the draining board by the sink, a jar of coffee and a packet of tea bags on the worktop. Eric noted with amusement that the tea was the same brand of jasmine flavoured green tea that he used himself. "Either Mister Jones was expecting me, or his taste is getting better," he thought. The kettle was empty, so he filled it at the sink and set it to boil. The other room he quickly discovered was the bathroom. Some of Sheila's make up lay on the window ledge and he frowned. Some ash from the hearth remained on his fingers, so to rinse them clean Eric twisted the cold water tap. Nothing happened. He tried the hot tap, and a small trickle of water came out. Quickly he rubbed his fingers together under the water and turned the tap off. There was a hand towel hanging over the radiator so Eric used that to dry his hands and then hung the towel on the edge of the bath.

Back in the kitchen the kettle had boiled, and steam had misted the kitchen window. Eric made some green tea and took the mug back to the living room. As he turned into the living room from the corridor, Eric heard a noise behind him. Turning around he could see nothing and so decided to investigate. He passed the kitchen; a glance through the open door showed him nothing. He moved on and looked into the bathroom. The cold tap was now pouring water into the hand basin at such a rate that the water was splashing out and overflowing onto the floor. Eric quickly reached out and turned the tap off. The water in the basin gurgled and flowed out down the waste pipe. The floor had not flooded, but was very wet. He took the hand towel from the side of the bath and dropped it onto the wettest patch of the floor. After carefully putting his tea down beside the door, Eric mopped up the water with the towel, squeezing the excess out into the bath until the floor was merely damp. The wet towel he hung back on the radiator.

"Tea!" he said to himself. But his mug of tea was not where he had left it. Slowly Eric peered around the door. A line of wet footprints led away from the bathroom door, clearly visible on the varnished wood of the corridor. The footprints turned into the living room. Eric followed them, noting that he himself left no marks on the floor even though he had been standing on the wet bathroom floor. His mug of tea was set, still steaming, on the coffee table but the living room was empty and the fire was out. The thin stream of smoke arising from the ashes told Eric that the fire was not yet completely lost. With the aid of two more unused sheets of Sheila's notepad he was able to restart the fire without too much trouble. He knelt before the grate until the fire had fully taken hold, and added more wood until the blaze and the heat satisfied him.

Leaving the fire, Eric sat down on one of the two couches and picked up his mug of tea. Outside the house a wind arose and began to moan softly in the eaves of Clyffe House and in the corridor, one of the bedroom doors creaked open and slammed shut again. Eric sighed. "I'm drinking my tea in peace," he said aloud. "This isn't scaring me, just annoying me." The door slammed shut again, and this time Eric heard slow footsteps in the hallway. In the hope of seeing something Eric left his tea and jumped up. As he looked out into the corridor he thought he caught a glimpse of someone going into the very end bedroom as the door closed firmly. He ran down the hall and tried the door that had just closed, but again it refused to open however hard he pulled at it. Then all the lights in the house went out. Exasperated, Eric tried the other two bedroom doors to no avail. All refused to open or to move. Walking back to the living room, Eric stopped by the front door and tried to open that. The front door refused to budge as well and Eric frowned, uneasy and concerned, as he realised that he was trapped inside the haunted cottage. He turned away from the front door to the living room and looked around. The fire was still burning brightly, and his tea was untouched where he had left it. Something was different though. Despite Eric's long experience he felt a cold chill as he realised that the walls were now clean. In the short time he had been out in the corridor, all the writing had vanished from the walls of the living room.

Discomforted, Eric walked to the wall beside the fireplace. He ran his open palm over the wall, but could feel nothing except the sense of age from the ancient house. Slowly however as he continued to touch the wall, that sense of age diminished and was replaced by other emotions. At first Eric could sense rage and anger and bitterness, feelings that were strong enough to make him stagger. Although he shook and his long hair stood away from his head as energy poured through him, he put his other hand on the wall for support and felt the feelings subside, to be replaced now by such sadness and loss and loneliness that Eric let out a sob of distress. A voice thundered in his head: **We are trapped here until it dies. Kill it, save us.** At once the feelings stopped and Eric was left leaning against the wall with his hair in disarray. Pushing himself upright, he staggered back to the couch and half fell onto it. His hand shook as he picked up his mug of tea, but then stilled as he forced himself to become calm again.

He could hear heavy footsteps outside in the yard, approaching the front door. Eric pulled the sports bag across the floor to his feet and struggled urgently with the zip until the bag was open. He delved inside the bag, and his hand closed on the weapon he sought. Then the door itself shook, and the latch rose and fell loudly. The sound of the wind rose, and the door handle was violently shaken until the front door finally surrendered and fell open to the dark night outside and to the intruder.

Chapter six

I jumped up from the couch to face the invaders. "Who are you?" I demanded.

The three men walked into the living room in silence, but then to my surprise stopped before they reached me. I backed away towards the rear wall of the room to put some space between the three men and me. I found their silence as intimidating as their presence. All three were large, heavily built men, dressed in similar though not identical black clothing. They did not look around the room, as would have been natural, but focused directly and exclusively on me.

Then a fourth man walked through the door behind them. I looked up hopefully in case he represented rescue. I recognised Mr Davis, and started forward; but saw then that he was dressed in the same way as the other three. He stopped beside them and smiled at me.

"Mister Jones." He spread his arms in a genial gesture.

"Mr Davis? What is going on?" I asked.

Mr Davis stared around the room and made several disapproving noises. "I do prefer my tenants to take better care of this cottage, Mister Jones. Look at all this lipstick on the walls!"

"I didn't do that, Mr Davis."

"Really?" Mr Davis sounded disbelieving, and I suppose that I couldn't blame him. I watched him raise one hand and run a finger down one wall, smearing the letters. He examined the red mark on his hand, sniffed it and then slowly licked his finger. His expression showed distaste.

"And Sheila didn't either."

"So who did?" asked Mr Davis.

"I don't know. It was rather spooky."

"Spooky?" Mr Davis raised his red-stained finger. "Lipstick," he remarked, conversationally. "Wouldn't you have thought that it would have been blood? So much more conventional. Somehow more satisfying, don't you think?"

I did not know what to make of that remark, but considered it somewhat ominous.

"So, you've left a bit of a mess. Well, the cleaners will cope with that before the next tourists."

"The next tourists?"

"Only booked it for a week, didn't you? Shame you won't be getting full value, isn't it?"

"You can't throw me out. First, Sheila has vanished and might be hurt somewhere. Second all our stuff is in here. Third, we've done nothing wrong." My attempt at bluster was not very good and certainly wasn't very successful. Mr Davis chuckled warmly at me.

"Well, as far as the third one is concerned it's not good guests who write stuff all over the walls in lipstick, is it Mister Jones? And I rather think that your Miss Balsam simply ran off with a man she met."

One of the three men who had first entered the house started to snigger. Mr Davis turned on him with a fierce glare, and he reverted at once to his earlier impassivity. "Mister Jones, I'm going to have to insist that you cut your break short." Mr Davis was terse, though not unpleasant.

"Well, It's your property, Mr Davis. I suppose I have to agree. I'll go and pack." I felt dispirited, but unsure that I had any right to argue as Sheila had booked the accommodation, not me. I started to walk towards the front of the living room with the intention of going to my bedroom to start packing.

"That won't be necessary." Mr Davis was still matter of fact and I felt very confused. Mr Davis beckoned to two of his companions, and they jumped forward and grabbed me by the arms.

"Hey! Let go!" I shouted. "What do you think you are doing? I've just said I was going!"

"Coming, not going, I'm afraid," said Mr Davis. He reached into his pocket and took out a set of rather shiny handcuffs.

I looked at them in shock. "What's this?" I demanded.

The two large men shook me rather roughly and then forced my arms out in front of me. Mr Davis smiled and snapped the handcuffs onto my wrists. They were only cheap, probably bought from some strange online shop, but served to hold my wrists tightly. One of the men then produced a thick piece of rope tied in a noose and slung it around my neck. My incipient anger drained away to be replaced by a growing and bowel-loosening fear.

"Why are you doing this?" I shouted.

"Bring him outside, Emlyn," ordered Mr Davis, ignoring me.

I staggered as the noose was jerked hard and for a moment I was choked as the rope tightened about my throat. My breath rasped painfully in my throat and I raised my handcuffed hands to pull the rope away from my windpipe. I gasped for air, and Mr Davis chuckled.

"That's what I like to see. Just be a good boy, bach, and do what you are told." Mr Davis turned on his heel and walked out of Clyffe House. Emlyn followed him, and after he again jerked viciously on the noose around my neck, I followed them out into the yard. Behind me I heard the front door of the cottage close, but was unable to do more than follow Mr Davis and my captor as they strode across the yard. Mr Davis went through the gate and turned to his right. I felt a moment of relief that I was not to be taken back to the fort and dragged up the hillside path, perhaps to the cave that I had glimpsed earlier.

Emlyn kept a constant pressure on the noose about my neck, and I tried to keep up with his pace. I stumbled and fell on the rough surface of the lane. My hands were cut and my knees hurt where I had fallen, unable to use my hands properly to cushion my landing on the uneven, unyielding stones; but not as much as the fire that burnt in my throat where the noose had tightened about my neck. Emlyn did not at first slacken his pace, and I was dragged after him. Lights spun in front of my eyes and my vision blurred but then Emlyn stopped and walked back to me. He kicked me viciously in the ribs.

"Now, now, Emlyn. There's no need for that," called Mr Davis. "I'm sure that our Mister Jones just fell over. Please don't hang him. Yet."

The pressure on the noose relaxed, and I gulped in great shuddering breaths of air. The air felt clean and sweet in my lungs but burnt in my throat. I tried to scream, but couldn't. Instead, I made a sobbing noise that alarmed me as much as the pain. Emlyn reached down and grabbed a handful of my clothing at the shoulder. He dragged me up without apparent effort and I scrabbled to get a footing in case he dropped me again. My hands tugged at the rope around my neck, and Emlyn punched me once in the stomach. I bent over, retching, and Emlyn laughed. He tugged again at the rope and walked on after Mr Davis. Stumbling on the uneven ground but desperate to keep my footing, I tried to walk within the tension of the rope so that it did not tighten again about my neck. I was convinced now that for reasons I did not understand they intended to hang me; but at that moment I could see no way for me to escape this awful fate.

Mr Davis opened the metal gate into the farmyard of Fferm Ffynnon and Emlyn dragged me inside. The gate was shut behind me, and in dread I looked up at the shell of the ruined house. The broken windows grinned down at me. I looked in fear at the building, and then in mounting terror at the trees that grew both around and inside the old farmhouse. I looked at Mr Davis, who was still smiling happily at me.

"What now?" I gasped. With a sudden determination I decided that if they were going to hang me I would at least resist to the last, as best I could. Emlyn was close in front of me with his back to me. I lifted my right foot and kicked him in the back of his left knee as hard as I could. He shouted and fell, but did not let go of the rope that held me. I pulled at the noose, trying to drag it over my head to get free while Emlyn jerked savagely at the end of the rope. Then Mr Davis was beside me and his genial manner had been replaced by a snarl.

"Pack it in right now Jones, or I'll make you suffer for it," he growled into my ear.

I stopped struggling. Emlyn got up and swung his right hand into my face in a mighty slap that knocked me to the ground, the noose again half strangling me. Emlyn hauled in the rope and I struggled to my knees, desperately dragging again at the noose with my fingers. Emlyn balled a huge fist and swung it at my face; but this time Mr Davis reached out. Although Emlyn was either a body builder or engaged in some manual occupation that had given him huge muscles, Mr Davis caught his wrist and held it without apparent effort.

"No, Emlyn," he said. "If he tries that again, he's all yours. But not this time."

"My leg hurts," Emlyn replied. He gave me a vicious look and using my small and dwindling reserve of courage, I returned it.

"What the hell is this about?" I demanded again.

"This way please," Mr Davis said to me politely, again ignoring my question.

I swore at him in reply. Emlyn jerked the rope and smiled nastily at me when I gasped in pain.

"Now, now, there's no need to be rude," Mr Davis told me.

I swore at him again.

"Bring him along, Emlyn. If he resists, there's no need to be gentle with him." Mr Davis turned away toward the outbuildings, away from the farmhouse. Emlyn and I followed after him in procession. None of the buildings looked to be in good condition or well used, but around one door the weeds had been trampled down. Mr Davis ignored that door and went past to the end of the building. I was led around the end of the low outbuilding and saw that behind it lay another long single story shed. This too was brick or stone built, with an old corrugated iron roof. The walls had been whitewashed once, but the colouring had long faded to a dirty shade of grey. Here, too, weeds grew in profusion both along the walls and in the passage between the buildings. The ground was still uneven, but I could walk more easily even with Emlyn tugging on the rope around my neck.

Mr Davis stopped at a metal sliding door. He took a bundle of rusty keys from one pocket and unlocked the padlock on the hasp. With an effort he slid the door open, and waved at Emlyn. Emlyn dragged me into the shed and Mr Davis followed me inside. He turned back and with an effort pulled the sliding door closed, and then pulled on a cord beside the door. That cord turned on the overhead fluorescent lights and I blinked in the sudden glare. The shed was oblong and roughly concreted on both floor and walls. There were no windows and almost no natural light. The room was completely empty and the walls were broken only in two places. In one corner the uneven wall had broken and cracked, and a grainy remainder of daylight filtered through the gaps where stones had fallen from the wall. In the wall that divided the long building was a pair of solid wooden doors, studded with black iron nails and held by long black hinges. These doors were heavily varnished and seemed to be the only maintained part of the building.

Mr Davis went over to the doors, and pulled them apart. There was nothing inside except a wall. He beckoned to Emlyn, who smiled nastily and jerked on the rope. My neck burned and I gasped with the pain. Emlyn grabbed me by one arm and threw me through the doors. I slammed into the wall and reeled back. Mr Davis grabbed my right arm, and spun me around as Emlyn walked up to me. He stood so close to me that I could smell his bad breath and took hold of me by the upper arms, holding me still. Mr Davis unfastened the handcuffs and Emlyn walked forward. Having no options I stepped backwards and Emlyn pushed me up against the stone wall. I realised that there was a gap, a tiny gap, between the doors and the wall and understood that it was their intention to imprison me there. I fought to get free, but I was no match for Emlyn's greater strength. Emlyn released his left hand and Mr Davis swung one door closed, casting part of that tiny space into shadow.

"Why?" I shouted desperately.

Mr Davis cocked his head to one side, and looked at me. He was clearly considering his reply. Then he shook his head. He reached for the other door.

"Don't do this! No!" I yelled. I thrust one leg forward to stop the door shutting on me, imprisoning me in that tiny closet but Emlyn stamped hard on my instep. With a grunt of pain, I moved my foot as a reflex action. The last thing I saw as Mr Davis slammed the other door closed upon me was Emlyn's triumphant leer. The darkness enfolded me with chinks of light showing at the edges and bottom of the door. I could hear mocking laughter from the room on the other side of the doors. I braced myself against the wall and pushed hard at the doors; they moved slightly and then were closed again.

"Drop that plank into those brackets," ordered Mr Davis. I could hear the sound of wood on wood. I again pushed with all my strength and although the doors moved a little they stayed firmly closed, shutting me in the tiny cell. Footsteps rang on the concrete floor, and I heard the sound of the metal door moving. Suddenly the glowing light around the frame around the doors went out and I was left entombed in absolute darkness, still with no idea why I had been taken and imprisoned. Or if I was ever to be released.

The space in which I had been imprisoned was very narrow. With some difficulty, by reaching my arms out to either side, I was able to bring my hands up close to my shoulders. I pushed as hard as I could on the doors, but although they moved slightly they were fastened too firmly for me to open. I stretched my arms out again and decided to explore the limits of my confinement. I could not touch a wall with either hand, so I shuffled carefully to the left. I suddenly realised with an oppressive horror that if I fell, or slumped to the floor in sleep, then in this narrow confine I would be unable to stand up again.

Then I froze. Underfoot something felt uneven. Carefully I lifted my foot and moved it; this time my foot touched something that rolled away into the darkness. I hooked my foot under whatever it was that I had trodden on, and tried to lift it. Reaching down as best I could in the cramped conditions, my fingers touched the object and with a shout of horror I dropped it. Even though I had never touched such a thing before, the feel of a human bone was unmistakeable. A chill ran through me as I realised that what had rolled away was the skull. Was this the

145

last occupant of this cell? Had he - or she - been left in this narrow confined prison until they had died and rotted to dust? How many others had Mr Davis done to death in this gruesome manner from the ancient horror tales?

Shrinking back from the remains, I shuffled to my right. After passing the doors I tentatively stretched out my right foot with a horrible foreboding. As I feared, before long my foot brushed other bones. Trapped in that absolute darkness I lacked the strength of will to cross those bones and see what lay beyond them; what if the narrow confine ran the length of the wall on both sides of the doors, and each side was filled with the decomposing remains of the previous prisoners?

The darkness, the narrow space, and the knowledge that I shared this confine with the remains of those made captive before me pressed down on me and became oppressive. I could barely move forward and could not bend my knees. I started to find it hard to breathe, and began to pant. I am not especially claustrophobic, I think, certainly no more than most people. However being confined in this awful place, unable to see and barely able to move was rapidly becoming intolerable. My knees shook, and suddenly I felt that I could not stand up for a moment longer. My knees buckled and I started sobbing without shame. But of course, I could not fall forward or sit down. Slowly I felt myself falling sideways, which I realised with terror would be a prelude to my end. Once fallen I would be unable to stand upright again.

I gritted my teeth and forced myself to stand upright. But I realised all too clearly that in time fatigue would force me to fall. I could only hope that I should be driven insane before I fell asleep and fell sideways to my eventual ruin.

How long does it take for fear to drive a man from sanity? Horribly, I felt that I was about to have an unparalleled chance to find out. Desperately I tried crying out for help. I knew that no help would come, could come, for who knew that I had been imprisoned here? Suddenly I realised that with a terrible cruelty Emlyn and Mr Davis had left the rope, the noose, around my neck. How many others had been in this prison and had finally given in to madness and ended their lives quickly rather than face the terror of death by thirst and hunger?

Another sob: and I wondered how many days I could live without water. I seemed to recall that it was generally thought to be seven days. But I decided that it did not matter. I was not mentally strong enough to last so many days in these conditions without losing my reason, and before that time I concluded I would find some way of employing the noose and ending my pain. That way too would be awful. The thought of dying alone in this cloying and oppressive darkness was an appalling thing - yet my choices had been taken away from me in the most dreadful way.

Shaking I stepped to my left, half falling; I pressed my hands hard against the wooden doors and pushed myself back upright. This time when my left foot crunched onto the bones on the floor, I paid no attention. My world had narrowed to a small focus; how long could I withstand the darkness? With sudden resolution I raised my elbows and put my hands on the noose about my neck. With some difficulty I pulled it over my head and dropped it to the floor.

I might be driven mad by this torture, I decided, but I would not be driven to despair, or at least to such despair that I took the appalling decision to end my own life. Madness and death might well lie in store for me in this dreadful place, but I should try to combat such things. I concentrated my thoughts on the fact that my friend Eric was on the way to help me; and I had such confidence in Eric and his strange abilities that the idea that he might rescue me was not too far-fetched. With a new resolution I strove to maintain my mental balance and maintain some composure.

I glanced down at the floor and pushed the noose further away from me with my foot. With a shock I realised that I had been able to see the noose. The darkness was not so absolute as it had been and the return of some vision encouraged me and raised my spirits. A sliver of light came onto the floor below the bottom of the doors. The lights in the room beyond my cell had been turned on.

Footsteps then, I heard footsteps crossing the room. Perhaps the time in the darkness had made my hearing more acute? I could, I decided, quite definitely hear footsteps and they were getting closer to the doors. I raised both hands, and hammered my palms on the wooden doors.

"Shhh!" came a whispered command from the other side of the doors. "Shhhh!"

I obeyed, in the very real hope that somehow Eric had already found me. There was a subdued scraping noise as my saviour dragged the wooden bar from the restraining brackets. The doors swung open under the pressure of my hands and body and I fell forward. I was grabbed before I hit the ground, and I clutched at my rescuer. The light in the room hurt my eyes and I had to squint against the glare, but I could see that his dark clothing was not of the sort Eric habitually wore.

"Shhhh!" he whispered again. "Let's not be heard! We need to get away quietly."

I wasn't going to argue with that. Despite the light I forced my eyes open, and looked at my rescuer. With a start, I recognised one of the three men who had entered Clyffe House with Mr Davis. "What are you doing?" I asked.

"Getting you out of here," he replied. "I'm Alwyn. Let's get you back to Clyffe House to get your stuff, then you can get out of here alive."

"But my friend, Sheila? What about her?"

Alwyn looked down at me, as I struggled to get back onto my feet. "We'll not get her out. Not now. But I can get you away."

"I'm not sure I want to go without my friend," I objected.

"Mr Jones. There's quite a lot of us, and one of you. There's nothing you can do for her."

"You could help me? Couldn't you? I can't just... abandon her."

"You can if you want to live. You've no idea what's going on here or what you are dealing with."

"That may be so, but..."

Alwyn interrupted me. "Come with me if you want to live," he said in a manner I considered to be rather melodramatic. He pulled me to my feet and helped me towards the far end of the room. I looked up as I became less unsteady on my feet and saw that the broken wall had been pulled down a little further. Enough stones had been removed to allow an exit to be made from the building. Alwyn pulled at my arm and his sense of urgency filtered through to me. I hurried across the room and only stopped when he prevented me from diving headfirst into the hole in the wall.

"Wait," he hissed. To my surprise, he left me and ran back to the prison. He closed the thick wooden doors and replaced the bar in the brackets, before coming back to me. "Now," he whispered, "if Iuan Davis comes in he will think you are still inside and not be looking for you outside. Get me?"

I nodded. Alwyn dropped to his knees and pushed his head and shoulders through the hole in the wall.

"All clear," I heard him say. He wriggled through the gap, his feet kicking with the effort. "Arms and head first!" he told me. I followed him through the hole and as I came out, he grabbed my arms and pulled my body through. I landed in a patch of nettles and tried hard not to complain, in case he thought I was ungrateful.

I looked round and saw that we were at the very back of the Fferm Ffynnon outbuildings. Alwyn pulled at my arm and I followed him into the small copse of trees. In the early night, we would be hard to see.

"I'll get you back to Clyffe House, and then you can get away in your car," he said quietly.

I was not at all keen on the idea as I felt that I would be abandoning Sheila, but this was not the time to start arguing. After all, Mr Davis with his collie could be around at any time and while Mr Davis would probably not be able to see us, his collie would certainly smell me and alert his owner. Alwyn led me to the wall at the end of the property and helped me to climb over. The wall was about six feet high but was made of rough and unevenly laid stone, and I could get a foothold and pull myself to the top with his help. We jumped down into the lane and I relaxed a little. We both looked up and down the lane, but it was deserted.

"Come on," he whispered to me, and set off up the lane towards Clyffe House. At the metal gate to Fferm Ffynnon he stopped and peered cautiously around the wall. "Come on," he said again. As I passed the gateway I glanced into the farmyard, and shivered at the sight of the ruined house that loomed across the decaying outbuildings. The wind had risen and the trees moved against the building, conveying a sense of unease and threat. Alwyn strode on as quickly as he could and I hurried as best I could to keep up with him. At the gate to Clyffe House, he stopped.

"You're on your own now," he told me. "Don't hang about, just get out of here."

"Where are you going?" I asked him.

He nodded towards the end of the lane and the frowning bulk of the hillfort. "The ceremony will start before long. If I'm not there, then..."

"Then what, Alwyn?"

"Then I'll be missed. Don't want that."

"Alwyn, thank you. Thank you for rescuing me. Thank you. But tell me, why? Why did you do it?"

He looked at me, his expression unreadable in the darkness. "There were some bones in there with you, weren't there?"

"Yes."

"That was my dad."

I didn't know what to say, I was so shocked. He turned away from me, and walked into the dark night. At the end of the lane, light flared, and torches flickered at the base of the hillside, and Alwyn quickened his pace. I watched until his dark clothing made it impossible to see him, then turned to the cottage. As I walked into the yard, I heard doors banging inside the house, although I could see no lights. Whatever walked in Clyffe House was clearly agitated, and I felt no small reluctance to brave its dangers. Yet I had not actually been hurt, merely very scared, inside Clyffe House. I waited in the yard until silence fell and then drew upon what small remainder of courage I had. If I were to escape, or even if I were to make another attempt to find my missing friend, I had to get things from the house. My wallet, her phone, Sheila's car keys, our house keys; all these things I wanted in my possession.

Knowing that if I did not act now I would lose the nerve to enter Clyffe House again, I went across the yard to the front door. The door refused at first to open, and with a sudden burst of anger I rattled the door handle until it gave way. I drew a deep breath, and flung open the door. Inside the living room I could see a figure on the couch - was this ghost or human? Friend or enemy? There was only one way to know, so I stood in the entry to the living room and making my voice sound as fearsome as I could through my bowel-loosening fear, I shouted: "Don't move!"

"Hello, Mister Jones," replied Eric.

*

Eric stood up, still holding onto his cup of tea. "Shut the door against the weather," he suggested.

I turned and did as he suggested. "Why are you sitting here in the dark?" I asked him.

"You might at least have said 'hello', first!" Eric replied. He sat down on the couch again, his face lit only by the shifting glow from the fire. "The lights all went out," he explained.

"They do that," I agreed. "I'll check the fuse box." As I expected, the main switch had tripped or been tripped, and I reached up to turn the power back on. As I touched the box, my hand was seized by an abrupt and intense cold, and I snatched it back, away from the fuse box in shock. "It's only cold!" I told myself, and lifted my hand again. The cold was so strong that it almost paralysed my hand, but I forced my fingers to lift the main power switch and the lights in Clyffe House came back on. I walked back into the living room and warmed my hand in front of the fire.

"What are you doing?" asked Eric.

I explained about the intense cold, and he understood at once.

"This house is troubled," he said.

"I guessed that when I woke up next to a skeleton," I told him. "Have you been in any of the other rooms?"

"Just the kitchen and the bathroom," he told me. "I couldn't open the other doors."

"That happened with us too. Then there was all this writing on the walls here." I looked around the room. "I suppose Mr Davis, the owner, has had it cleaned it off after he dragged me off and tried to kill me."

Eric put down his tea and looked at me in surprise. "Seriously?"

"Oh yes," I told him. I now felt very cold indeed and put more wood on the fire.

"Right, Mister Jones, please tell me everything. From the start."

I sat down on the other couch, and started the story. I related how we had come here to allow Sheila time to write her book.

"I assume these are her notes?" asked Eric, pointing to the sheets and sheets of notepaper on the end of the couch he was using.

"Yes. And her laptop should be here somewhere, too."

Eric glanced around the living room. "No, I haven't seen a computer anywhere."

"That's odd. Maybe it was taken away when I was. Anyway, we found it a bit hard to get into the bedrooms that first night."

"I can understand that. None of the doors would open for me just now, as if they were locked - yet none of the doors have anything but a simple latch." Eric deliberately did not mention the door that had yawned open for him in invitation.

"We did get the doors to open in the end, and after we'd gone to sleep I felt someone get into bed with me. I woke up and put the light on and there was a skeleton lying there. Then we had trouble with the lights and Sheila had messages written to her in steam on the windows."

"What messages?" asked Eric.

"Always the same one. 'Help me'. In fact, after she vanished it was written in her lipstick all over these walls." I looked around at the walls, now innocent of any writing at all.

"I saw those," agreed Eric, "although the words read 'help her' when I saw them."

"You saw them? I suppose Mr Davis had the walls cleaned then when he hauled me off."

"No, Mister Jones. They were here when I came, and vanished while I was here."

I shivered. Even with Eric here I was still frightened of being in this house. "We should leave," I said abruptly. "What if Davis comes back, or finds that I've escaped and comes looking for me?"

"Why did he want to kill you?" asked Eric, looking completely unflustered by this news.

"I've no idea. I had told him that Sheila had gone missing, and was insistent on looking for her."

"Then that is probably the reason," suggested Eric. "There is something deeply disturbing happening here, Mister Jones. Sheila has got caught up in it, and so have you."

"This house... this house seems linked to it all?"

"Has anything else happened to you?" asked Eric.

"Yes, last night. I was trying to go to bed. I couldn't make the door to my room open."

"Which room is yours?" asked Eric.

"There are three doors at that end of the corridor. The one on the left is mine, the one on the right, next to the living room, is Sheila's. We didn't use the one in the middle as we couldn't open the door. But then last night it was the only door I *could* open. The lights had gone out and I couldn't see a thing. I walked in trying to find the bed, and suddenly the floor gave way and I slid down into a tunnel."

"Did you indeed," said Eric.

"Yes. The tunnel led away towards the hill at the end of the lane. At the end of the tunnel was some weird cave with a pool in the middle and an altar at one end. It was empty, so I tried another tunnel and found it came out on the hillside down that way." I waved vaguely at the end of the lane and Eric looked very thoughtful.

"The house tried to get me to go into that room," he told me. "I didn't, which rather sounds like a wise decision now. What next?"

"Well, I made my way back here and found Sheila had gone. But she had left things here she would always have taken if she had walked out or gone somewhere of her own accord."

"Yes," agreed Eric. "Her mobile phone, her makeup, her handbag."

"Exactly. So I went out looking for her. Couldn't find her anywhere, told Mr Davis when I met him, but he wasn't concerned at all and suggested she had run off with someone, which is ridiculous."

"Hum."

"Then when I made it clear I wasn't leaving, he turned up here with three big blokes and dragged me off."

Eric leant forward and put his cup of tea down. "Where to?" he asked.

"The farm along the lane. Fferm Ffynnon, it's called. The farmhouse itself is a ruin but the outbuildings still stand. In one of them there was sort of a prison. Really narrow, a hole in the wall really, with big wooden doors. Davis shoved me in there in the darkness, and locked the doors. I don't think he was coming to let me out."

"And yet here you are, Mister Jones. You do have a talent for escaping from tight scrapes, do you not?"

"Me? Well this time, I was rescued by one of the men who had captured me." I rubbed the angry red mark on my throat. "He told me his father had been subjected to that way of being killed and that was why he was letting me out. I should now get away he told me, and said that I'd never see Sheila again. Then he went off towards the hill. He didn't really say, but it looked to me as if there was to be a meeting there."

"I wonder," said Eric. "A meeting or a ceremony?"

One of the fire irons fell over with a loud crash, sending sparks from the fire flying into the air. We both turned to look at it.

"I wonder," repeated Eric, and then was quiet.

"If whatever is happening here is connected?" I asked.

The fire blazed suddenly, as the wind roared outside. Inside the house, there was a loud noise from the corridor as one of the bedroom doors opened, slammed shut and opened again. I stood, and peered cautiously out of the living room. The door of the middle bedroom stood wide open. Smoke billowed out from the fire, making us both cough. When it cleared, the wall above the fire was defaced by writing made from the soot and ash: **HELP ME…..HELP HER** it read. **RELEASE US… HELP HER**.

"Well," said Eric cheerfully, "that's a clear enough message isn't it, Mister Jones?"

I nodded grimly. The message was clear enough.

Eric reached for his sports bag. "Once more into the breach, and all that," he said to me.

"Eric, what are we going to do, exactly?"

"Mister Jones, I have no idea. Do you know who - or what - has taken Sheila? Has taken the life of whoever is trapped here? Or where she has been taken?"

"No, Eric. But I've a horrible feeling that we will find the answers to those questions in that chamber at the end of the tunnel below that bedroom."

As if in confirmation, the door in the corridor slammed shut again, then creaked open ominously. Eric opened the zip of his sports bag. Inside I could see the handles of swords that I knew from past experience he had crafted himself from silver in a workshop he had created in his garage. He took two powerful torches from the bag and tossed one across the room to me. I fumbled the catch but managed to hold onto the torch rather than drop it. Eric closed the zip on his sports bag and got to his feet.

"Turn the lights out," he told me. "Because you are supposed to have left, isn't that so? Or been fastened up to die?"

I nodded.

"So there's no one in here is there, Mister Jones. If lights are on in this building, and anyone looks out towards this cottage, what will they think?"

Of course, Eric was right. I went back to the fuse box. Cautiously I reached for the mains switch. As I did so it tripped out and all the lights failed. I shivered with both cold and fear. While it seemed probable that whatever spirit haunted this house presently intended no harm, its very existence - demonstrated in such a forceful manner - was frightening.

"This way," called Eric softly. I joined him at the entrance to the living room. The hallway was very dark, but there was just enough light to see that one of the bedroom doors was open. Eric turned on his torch and shone the beam down the corridor. We could see that the door to the middle bedroom was open. Carefully we advanced to the door, Eric leading and me close behind his left shoulder. Eric shone his torch into the room, but it failed to pierce the darkness.

"This is the bedroom where you fell down into the tunnel?" asked Eric softly.

"Yes. This is how it was when I went in. So dark I couldn't see a thing."

"Switch on your torch too, Mister Jones."

I flicked the switch on the torch. When it was pointed at the floor, the beam was bright and clear. However, when I lifted the heavy torch to direct the beam into the bedroom it failed to penetrate beyond the doorway.

"What exactly did you do, then?" asked Eric.

"I could see the bed ahead of me. The floor was dark, but I thought I could see a rug. When I walked in I couldn't see a thing, and then I was sliding down a steep slope."

"Not a drop, then?"

"No, Eric. Definitely a slope. But steep, too steep to easily climb back up."

"Right, then." Eric strode forward into the bedroom. I heard him gasp.

"Eric? Are you all right?" I called, trying to keep my voice down.

"Of course I am, Mister Jones. As you said, it is a slide, not a drop. Are you coming?"

This was of course another test of my courage. It did seem to me that part of my personality was undergoing much more testing than normal. My daily life is rather sedate and this continuous action and drama was beginning to take a heavy toll on me. I had fallen down that slide into the low, dark tunnel before and I knew that the only way out would lead through the chamber below the hill; now occupied, I presumed, by people who had already tried to kill me today.

"Well?" I thought that Eric's tone was a little sharp and that stung me into action. Squaring my shoulders I stepped into the bedroom, waiting for the floor to vanish below my feet as it had before. Instead I banged my shins on the frame of the bed and, losing my balance, fell forward onto the mattress.

"Eric? Eric?"

There was no reply. I swung the torch around, and now the beam illuminated the floor and a woven rug. Of the slope that led to the tunnel below the floor there was no sign. In frustration I stood on the rug and jumped up and down. Perhaps it was my imagination, but I felt that the floor shook slightly. I dropped to my hands and knees and felt desperately around for a join or a catch in the floor that would allow me to release the floor and drop down to join Eric.

I was startled by a bang on the floor from below. I knocked back, twice. Again there was a knock from below. I presumed that Eric was managing to either reach the roof of the tunnel or was banging on the wooden floor with something, probably his torch. Seized by a sudden inspiration I rolled over and got up. I walked out into the long hall and closed the bedroom door. I counted to five and then opened the door again and walked firmly into the room, holding my breath. Once again I painfully barked my shins against the bed, swearing loudly in frustration. I jumped up and down on the rug, but to no avail.

"Eric! Eric!" I yelled. There was no reply, and so I sat down on the bed to think. Eric had evidently come to the conclusion that Sheila was going to be involved in, or subjected to, some horrid ceremony; probably in that chamber I had found hidden within the hillside. He was now trapped within that tunnel, his only way out through that cave. However fearful I was, my only choice was clear - I had to try and get into the chamber myself.

The only way I knew was to climb the side of the hill, and see if I could find that narrow fissure into the hillside. I walked back to the living room with the aid of my torch. The fire was still burning brightly, and I put even more wood on the flames.

A weapon would be nice, I thought. Annoyingly, I knew that Eric carried two silver swords in his sports bag - which, like Eric, was no longer accessible to me. What else could I use as a weapon? I looked around the living room and inspiration struck. I picked up the iron poker and, feeling vaguely ridiculous, pushed it through the belt in my trousers. It hung there awkwardly and banged annoyingly against my leg when I moved, yet its weight and feel were reassuring. I had discovered before that both human and supernatural creatures had a strongly rooted objection to being struck by a length of cold iron; the poker would have to suffice.

Leaving the house, I glanced nervously at the remains of Fferm Ffynnon. A small light flickered amongst the ruins and my heart froze; who would be amongst those old buildings at this time of night? No one, I was sure, who would wish me well. With increased caution I hurried across the yard to the gate into the lane. Peering round the wall I could see no one at all, and felt rather foolish. I set off towards the hill fort. Several times on the lane I felt an overpowering sensation that I was being watched. Although I spun around several times, on no occasion did I see anyone or anything behind me, and eventually put the feeling down to being nervous. As I approached the gateway to the track leading up the side of the hill, a stone rattled behind me and I froze. That had sounded frighteningly like a footfall on the uneven surface. The wind moaned in the trees beside the road, and the branches shifted, casting unsettling shadows across the lane, across the walls - and across me. I put my right hand on the end of the iron poker, ready to use the weapon for my self-defence. The hairs on the back of my neck rose and a cold shiver ran down my spine. Slowly this time I turned around. The lane was empty. I could not decide if that was more frightening than seeing a pursuer and found that I was sweating with a combination of fear and anxiety.

The gate was unlocked so I pushed it open and stepped through. Looking around, my attention was caught by a dark, lumpy patch of ground to one side. I knelt down, and my hand touched not earth, but a groundsheet or some other rubberised fabric. I felt around until I had found a corner, or an edge, and lifted the sheeting. In the light of my torch I could see some empty bags, a can of petrol that proved to be mostly full and a box of matches. I shoved the matches in my pocket and looked at the petrol can thoughtfully. Taking it was a simple decision, and a moment later I was walking cautiously along the path that rose up the side of the hill - my torch in one hand, the petrol can in the other, and the poker returned to my belt. Part way up the slope I heard the unmistakeable sound of the hinges on the gate creaking. Again, when I turned the torch on the gateway, I saw nothing and was again more disturbed by that than if I had seen someone, Mr Davis perhaps, coming to seek me out. From my vantage point I could see along the lane to Clyffe House and Fferm Ffynnon, but the lights that been in evidence earlier had gone out.

I carried on up the footpath. At the top, I stepped off the path awkwardly and climbed down into the defensive ditch dug all those centuries of time ago. No longer a deterrent, even to an unfit and middle-aged man like myself, the remains of the ancient fortifications still carried a sinister air in the dark night. I peered upwards, but the moon was not yet in view. The ground here was uneven and I needed to pay close attention to the small pool of light cast by my torch to avoid falling. After a short walk I came upon the stone that marked the entrance to the passage, and then I saw the large bush that I recalled had disguised the entrance to the underground chamber. It had been pulled to one side and not properly replaced. I put down the petrol can and pulled the bush away from the tunnel entrance. The narrow slit in the hillside looked ominous, and I needed a real effort of will to force myself through the gap until I encountered the passage itself. I looked back, but the exit was dark, the sky outside offering no light to guide or help me. Suddenly the tunnel was full of sound. I listened carefully, but the repeated phrases *'Assanc, Addanc, Addanc, Assanc'* meant nothing to me. With a heavy heart and fear in my mouth, I crept down the tunnel towards the chamber.

Eric slid down the tilted floor and landed in an ungainly heap at the bottom of the slope. Rubbing his leg, he stood upright and frowned as he hit his head on the low roof of the tunnel. "This will be Mister Jones' tunnel, then," he muttered. He swung his torch around, and saw the walls and the confining roof of his surroundings. The tunnel led away from him in two directions. One he knew led to the underground chamber Mister Jones had described to him: the other he assumed must lead to Fferm Ffynnon. But which was which? Eric clambered to his feet, and shone the torch back up the slope towards the bedroom of Clyffe House. The tunnel roof rose to admit the sloping floor, but otherwise was solid. There was no opening, nothing to reveal how he had entered this tunnel - and certainly nothing to suggest that Mister Jones could follow him down. He tried to climb up but the slope was too steep for him so he reached upwards with his torch and knocked on the roof of the tunnel. He shouted for Mister Jones, who had after all been close behind him when he entered the dark bedroom, but could hear nothing in reply. No light other than his torch lit the tunnel and reluctantly at last he sat back down on the floor beside his sports bag.

"Ah well," he said aloud. "It won't be the first time I've been alone, or without assistance. And a lady needs rescuing. Now, which way?" The tunnel led away in both directions. "A sign would, of course, be too much to hope for," Eric mused. He closed his eyes, and concentrated; but could hear nothing. At last he swept the beam of his torch around the floor and paused when something caught his eye. He dropped to his knees and crawled a few feet away from the slope leading down from Clyffe House. "Footprints," he muttered, peering at the floor in the light of the torch beam. "Footprints. But whose are they?" Eric sat back on his heels and thought. He could see faint footprints leading away down the tunnel to his left. But were these the prints made by Mister Jones as he found his way to the underground chamber with the pool and the altar, or were they the prints of someone else returning from there?

Eric took a breath, and with a small prayer to Vishnu, struck out in the direction he finally considered to be best. The tunnel roof was low and he had to stoop. Before long his back began to ache, and he paused for a rest. He sat with his back to one wall and assumed the meditation position that he found so comfortable before relaxing. After a few moments, Eric raised his head and shone his torch around the tunnel. He could see nothing other than the continuous rough walls and low ceiling stretching into the darkness in both directions, but he could sense something different, a change in the atmosphere. He strained his senses: there it was, a suspicion of an air movement on one cheek. Not strong enough to be a breeze, just a stirring in the otherwise dead air within the tunnel. He breathed carefully and thought that he could detect a hint of salt, a freshness, the scent of the sea.

The torchlight revealed nothing but Eric was convinced that somewhere close was another passageway, one that led to the sea. He rose to a crouch, picked up his sports bag and went carefully down the tunnel, seeking the source of the fresh air. The faint breeze grew a little stronger, then faded. Had he missed the opening? Eric ran the beam from the torch carefully around the tunnel, looking to his front - he could see nothing. Then he turned back the way he had come and smiled. On one wall, there was a small gap, concealed by the way the wall curved and impossible to see from the other direction. It was just large enough for Eric to squeeze through, so he did. Once through the entry he looked ruefully at his suit, which was now covered in stains from the wall. The smell of the sea was much stronger, the tunnel roof higher, and he was able to walk more easily. Suddenly the tunnel turned two corners and the sound of waves crashing onto rocks boomed loudly into the tunnel. Eric smiled and walked carefully to the end of the tunnel. The opening was half way down a cliff and Eric swayed giddily, grabbing the wall for support as he almost overbalanced. Fifty feet below his lofty perch, the hungry waves crashed and roared on the jagged rocks. He looked out across the wide expanse of Cardigan Bay and laughed.

Kneeling on the lip of the tunnel, Eric examined the cliff. He nodded in satisfaction when he saw a narrow and crumbling flight of steps cut into the rock face, leading upwards towards the top of the cliff. "I saw the sea," he said aloud before turning back to the dark passage behind him. Knowing that there was a possible escape route gave him more confidence and he walked purposefully toward the main tunnel, hoping that the batteries in his torch would hold out. Once again he pushed through the narrow opening and without hesitation turned to his left. Ducking his head to avoid knocking his scalp on the roof was uncomfortable, but he persevered.

Finally Eric checked his pace as he realised that he could hear voices ahead of him. He paused, and listened carefully.

"Assanc, Addanc, Addanc, Addanc, Assanc," he heard. Eric looked puzzled, then thoughtful. Then he frowned.

"I've heard that before," he muttered under his breath. "But where? Where? And when? Long, long ago." Carefully, Eric put his sports bag down on the floor of the tunnel and moved forward. When he turned off the torchlight he could see a faint red glow on the walls and floor of the tunnel. The tunnel itself curved to the right, and he inched carefully around the bend, keeping as close to the wall of the tunnel as he could. The tunnel ended in a set of ruined oaken doors that sagged open on the ancient hinges. Red light poured through the gaps in the timber. Eric crept forward to the doors and peered through. The tunnel had reached a large underground space, lit by a red light, which seemed stronger than could be expected from the four burning torches he could see fixed to the wall on the opposite side of the chamber above a low altar. A large pool surrounded by a painted and inscribed circle dominated the very centre of the room, and a huge and ornate chair stood to one side of the pool.

"Assanc, Addanc, Addanc, Addanc, Assanc," he heard again, and

he peered through a gap in the ruined door, squinting to his right. Eric could see a group of people standing together against one wall; they were the source of the chanting. As he watched they spread out and moved towards the pool in a loose line. In the centre of the line was one who was not chanting, and staring hard through the door he realised that it was Sheila Balsam, the girl he had come to save. Sheila did not seem to be tied or restrained by anything, but she was being held firmly by the wrists and forced to be part of the group.

"Assanc, Addanc, Addanc, Addanc, Assanc," the group continued to chant. As Eric watched a group of burly men came from somewhere out of his line of vision and joined the line, circling around the pool of water in the centre of the chamber.

"Assanc, Addanc, Addanc, Addanc, Assanc."

Eric counted quickly; he could now see twenty people plus Sheila surrounding the pool, all careful not to step on the painted circle that ran around the outside of the pool. Examining the circle as best he could through the assorted legs and feet, Eric could just make out various strange symbols inscribed on the floor; but although they seemed familiar in some way, he could not recall where he had seen them before. He tried to remember, but the memory eluded him. "It will come back to me," he said to himself and instead paid attention to the events inside the chamber.

"Assanc, Addanc, Addanc, Addanc, Assanc!" The chant echoed around the chamber, and the group gathered around the pool raised their voices until the echoes rang and rang and rang. *"Assanc, Addanc, Addanc, Addanc, Assanc."*

Eric heard Sheila cry out and then scream. He pushed gently at the broken wooden doors until they moved enough for him to be able to see clearly. The men surrounded the pool, but there were not enough of them for his view of the water to be entirely impeded.

"Assanc, Addanc, Addanc, Addanc, Assanc." The tone became triumphant, and Eric peered intently at the water. In his peripheral vision he could also see Sheila struggling violently and now being held firmly by two men who did not pause in their chanting.

"Assanc, Addanc, Addanc, Addanc, Assanc."

Sheila screamed so loudly that Eric winced, but he did not leave his vantage point. Then the still surface of the pool rippled.

"Assanc, Addanc, Addanc, Addanc, Assanc!" Now most of the group fell to their knees before the pool. Eric glanced across at Sheila: the only two men who were not on their knees were holding her tightly.

"Assanc, Addanc, Addanc, Addanc, Assanc!" The surface of the pool was broken and Eric turned his attention to the water. Slowly the crocodile-like head of the Addanc emerged from the pool, and with water dripping from his jaws the Addanc turned his head around to survey those present in his chamber. Unconsciously, Eric held his breath with the tension. When he had turned a full circle the Addanc moved to the side of the pool and raised himself from the water by climbing the short flight of steps beside the chair.

"Assanc, Addanc, Addanc, Addanc, Assanc." The chanting fell in tone and volume and became deeper and more reverential. Standing now on the side of the pool, with water draining from

his naked, stunted body, the Addanc again stared all around the circle. Finally he raised his arms and the group fell silent. Sheila screamed again, and the sound rang in the suddenly quiet chamber. The Addanc focused his gaze on her and then pointed at the ground by his feet. Her captors wrestled with Sheila as she resisted. The monster looked at her dispassionately.

"So," he said to Sheila. Eric watched the Addanc stare at her and run one hand over his jaws in a reflective manner. Sheila raised her head and Eric thought he saw fear replace the anger in her expression.

"You have chosen death, not life, and it remains only to decide how you die," announced the Addanc.

"No!" screamed Sheila, but the Addanc was unmoved.

"Death!" declared the Addanc, and the surrounding group echoed his order with a terrible cry. "Death! Death!"

Chapter seven

I crept down the tunnel towards the chamber at the end. I had no desire at all to go down that dark passage, but I had no doubt that Sheila was held captive there to face some awful fate and that it was my duty as her friend to go to her assistance. Unlike the underground passageway from Clyffe House, this tunnel was both taller and much shorter; I quickly made my way to the end and flattened myself against the wall.

"Assanc, Addanc, Addanc, Addanc, Assanc," came a deep chant from the chamber beyond the tunnel. I was perplexed. What could this mean? The chant was repeated. *"Assanc, Addanc, Addanc, Addanc, Assanc."* I pressed myself against the rock wall and moved forward until I could see into the chamber. A group of people stood in a ring against one wall. I could see only a few faces, but I recognised Mr Davis and Emlyn there amongst the chanting men. With a sigh of dread, I saw that Sheila was standing in the centre of the circle.

"Assanc, Addanc, Addanc, Addanc, Assanc." The circle split, and I could now see that Sheila was there unwillingly, for she struggled against the two men who held her arms firmly. *"Assanc, Addanc, Addanc, Addanc, Assanc."*

I had to admit to myself that I was frightened of these men. I had no idea what their purpose might be, or what their plans were for Sheila but I feared the worst for my friend. I have some limited experience of the paranormal, perhaps more than most people ever have in their lifetimes, and in that experience I have found that such scenarios are never planned with anything good or charitable in mind. While I can be ambivalent about the existence of evil as a force, I have no doubt at all that men are easily inclined to act in a way that rationally can only be described as evil; and that there are creatures in our universe that are not well inclined towards humanity as a breed.

"Assanc, Addanc, Addanc, Addanc, Assanc." Most of the group walked towards the water in the middle of the chamber, and the two heavily built men holding Sheila started to drag her towards the pool. My heart sank. Was their plan to drown my friend, perhaps to throw her living into that circle of water and watch in anticipation and delight as she struggled for her life before finally fading and sinking into the unknown depths? I shivered in horror at the thought. Sheila struggled wildly to free herself, but to no avail. I watched my friend pull in vain against the strong arms of her captors, watched her twist and jerk and fight as best she could.

"Assanc, Addanc, Addanc, Addanc, Assanc." The group spread out slowly around the pool, and Sheila - still resisting to the best of her ability - was dragged before the ornate chair that was placed by one side of the pool. *"Assanc, Addanc, Addanc, Addanc, Assanc."*

The sight transfixed me, and I was unable to drag my eyes away from the awful scene. As I watched in horror, I was unable to prevent a low moan escaping from my lips as the still waters of the pool began to ripple and stir. One of the men glanced back towards the tunnel in which I was hiding and I shrank back a little further out of sight, hoping to avoid detection. I was there to rescue Sheila, but at the moment I could not think of any plan or device by which I might accomplish this goal.

"Assanc, Addanc, Addanc, Addanc, Assanc." The tone of the

chant held a triumphant note, and I caught my breath as the waters stirred again and a nightmare horror from the ancient past rose from the pool and looked around the chamber. The monster fixed its gaze on Sheila and as much as those reptilian features could be said to have an expression, I thought that it looked both hungry and vengeful. The monster found some steps that were concealed from my sight below the waters, and rose slowly from the pool. Water dripped from its sparse, nude and truncated frame and I felt my gorge rise in my throat at the sight of the deformed body.

"*Assanc, Addanc, Addanc, Addanc, Assanc.*" The two men holding Sheila bowed to the monstrosity and threw Sheila down at its feet. She raised her head to stare at the creature, and I marvelled at her courage in not hiding her sight from the beast.

The monster hoisted itself into the chair and made itself comfortable. Its stunted feet did not reach the floor, yet somehow, when seated on that ornate chair it held an unexpected air of majesty. The group of men all turned to face the creature and bowed very low. "*Assanc, Addanc, Addanc, Addanc, Assanc,*" they repeated, then raised their heads and fell silent. The last of the water from the pool dripped from the crocodile jaws and fell to the floor of the chamber. The monster looked around the assembly with what I assumed was some satisfaction before turning its attention to Sheila, who lay still on the floor before its feet.

Surprisingly then, then monster spoke and I marvelled to hear clear English from that reptilian mouth. Then with horror I listened as the monster pronounced its sentence of death upon my friend. Appalled I heard the assembled men chant their approval for the murder.

"Followers of the Addanc, I greet you here in my realm within Prydain." I frowned, puzzled, until I recalled that Prydain had once been the name of this land and of the wider lands leading out from Wales through greater Britain. Was this creature that old, I wondered? Did it hail from a time before our history had begun to be written down? Although I do like to read some of the ancient stories of these lands, I had never heard of such a being as this.

"I have decided that the time has come," continued the Addanc, "for me to resume my place as the Lord of this Realm, and you who are my devoted followers shall assume your places below me but above your fellows." He looked down at Sheila and paused. How, I wondered, did this creature from a lost time hope to come out into the light of our modern times and wrest the rule of several counties from the Authorities? The Addanc looked away from Sheila and scrutinised his followers' faces. "I have planned against this day, and you have loyally aided me in my efforts." I followed his gaze and was surprised to see the expression on some of the faces around the pool. Not all were excited and enthusiastic at the idea that this demon from the past wished to rule in the present and future, yet for a reason I did not understand they seemed to be compliant and complicit in the plan.

"We have worked hard. All of us have striven to see this day, hoped for by generations of your folk, father to son, father to son, down generations you no longer count and at last the day is upon us."

The Addanc, ungainly with its deformed body and legs, got down from the chair. It stared at Sheila, who lay still before it, with an inscrutable expression. Then it turned away from her and began to pace around the pool, following the line of a circle that had been painted on the floor of the chamber around the waters. Was the circle symbolic, I speculated? Or did it serve some magical purpose? The Addanc walked slowly away from her, looking directly into the eyes of its followers as it went. Some held the gaze fearlessly and with resolution, others after a moment of that silent examination, dropped their heads.

As I watched the tableau, I saw Sheila suddenly tense, then spring to her feet and try to run from the dreadful pool. But the men closest to her had obviously been prepared for such an escape attempt, and before she had taken three steps they were upon her. Seizing her arms, they wrestled with her and forced her to turn back towards the monster. Apart from a brief glance, the Addanc had ignored the commotion and continued its slow progression around the pool, examining each man as he did so: to what aim or purpose I did not know. I presumed that he was in some psychic way testing the mettle and resolution of his followers. Her captors again forced Sheila to her knees in front of the ornate chair.

At length, the Addanc completed its stately circle and returned to the carved chair. It grasped the ornate arms of the chair and pulled itself back up. Once seated, it looked slowly around the chamber before turning its attention entirely upon Sheila.

"You," the Addanc said to her.

"Me, nothing!" retorted Sheila. "I'm no part of your plan!"

"You," replied the Addanc, "have no choice in the matter. My plan has been long in the making, long in the preparation, but will be swift in its execution."

"Execution?" asked Sheila, her tone uncertain. Clearly the word had some connotations she did not like.

"Yes, execution. For now I propose to return from the shadows and regain my power, the choice for your people will be clear and firm. To accept me as Lord, or to perish."

"Perish? You mean you'll kill people? You, on your own?" Sheila laughed at the Addanc, and I admired her bravery. "You'll last about two minutes when the army turns up. Then you'll be killed yourself, or more likely dragged off to a zoo."

Some of the assembled men made threatening noises, but the Addanc just laughed. "I think not." The Addanc opened its arm wide to embrace those around the pool. "I have decided that the long wait is over. You, my faithful followers, have waited for this moment for generations. Now, together we will leave this shadowed chamber and take our place in the sunlight of Prydain once again."

"Assanc, Addanc, Addanc, Addanc, Assanc," chanted the assembly, and the Addanc smiled.

"Where is Iuan Davis?" the Addanc asked.

I watched Mr Davis shake as if suddenly doused by cold water. Then he walked before the Addanc and dropped to his knees.

"Lord, what is your will?"

"You and yours have kept this secret place well for many years. I will not forget." The Addanc shuffled off the chair, and stood, deformed and monstrous before Mr Davis. "My plan has been well prepared, by you and our kin. Yes, our kin I say. For although my people have long since died out from this sorry world, leaving me alone to carry the memories of my race, you and yours have supported me for generations." It looked around the chamber. "This has been a poor place for one such as I, but it has been secret. The rites have been observed and you have arranged well for the necessary sacrifices."

I felt a wave of horror as I realised that the monster intended Sheila to be the next sacrifice. Sheila, on the floor before its feet, must have realised the same thing for she stirred. The Addanc looked at her dispassionately and then placed one foot on her back, holding her down. Sheila struggled, but the Addanc's weight was too much for her. The Addanc waved regally at Iuan Davis, who went and knelt immediately before it. Mr Davis bent forward, and when he then straightened, stood and turned around, I could see a yellowish liquid dribbling from his lips. He looked ecstatic; but below him Sheila vomited noisily. She struggled, but the Addanc's foot held her firmly pinned to the floor.

"Assanc, Addanc, Addanc, Addanc, Assanc." The assembly started their ritual chant again, as one by one the others of the group left their places around the pool and each in turn knelt before the Addanc to receive their obscene gift. I watched in revulsion, but could not help wondering what the point of this dreadful rite could be. At length it was over and Iuan Davis again knelt before his Master. The Addanc gave him a quiet instruction and Mr Davis nodded. I watched him walk from the poolside to the altar and pick up an object from the table. I could not see what it was, but when he turned back to return there was no mistaking the look of grim satisfaction on his face.

Where was Eric? That something dreadful was taking place here I had no doubt. Nor did I doubt now that Sheila was in mortal danger. While I am no action hero type, I also knew that I would be shamed for life if I made no attempt to rescue my friend. Breathing deeply, I wondered what I could possibly do against so many, and wished that Eric with his skills and weapons were beside me to help. I tried as hard as I could to screw up my courage to intervene even though I knew that to do so was hopeless. Mr Davis drew near to the Addanc, and I saw that he held a tall goblet of metal, chased and worked with images that I could not identify at such a distance. He bowed, and gave the Addanc the goblet. The Addanc raised it high in one hand; the crocodile jaws open to reveal many gleaming teeth.

"Assanc, Addanc, Addanc, Addanc, Assanc." The Addanc lifted his foot and bending down grabbed Sheila's hair with its free hand. Sheila was forced to her feet with her head tilted back. The Addanc raised the goblet to her lips. Sheila shook her head violently and the Addanc shifted its grip on her hair, holding it closer, tighter, and restraining her completely. With a sick feeling in my stomach I realised that this was the last moment left to me and I stepped away from the wall.

As I did so, I felt myself roughly seized from behind and shoved into the chamber. The Addanc paused, and Sheila twisted in its grip. She looked at me, and a terrible hope shone in her face for a moment, to be followed by shock and despair. I stumbled forward into the chamber and struggled to keep my balance. I looked over my shoulder and saw two more men I presumed were part of both the local farming community and this more secret and dreadful community below the ancient hill fort. They must have walked down the tunnel from the hillside behind me, and while my attention was fixed on the dreadful scene in the chamber, crept upon me from behind and then thrust me into the cave.

"What is this?" demanded the Addanc.

"Let her go!" I shouted.

There was a murmur of anger from the assembly that I had dared to raise my voice in this ancient place, but the Addanc seemed unmoved, or even amused. "How traditional," it said. "A lover, to the rescue, is that not so?"

"Run, Mister Jones!" gasped Sheila.

The Addanc shook her by the hair. "I'd appreciate your assistance by staying silent," it said to her. The crocodile jaws opened, and the monster's teeth brushed against Sheila's cheek. I could see her quiver, and felt a rage burn within me against this inhuman thing.

"Let her go!" I demanded again.

Behind me, one of the men who had surprised me laughed, coarsely. I took a step towards the monster and felt my arms grabbed and held firmly. Like Sheila a few minutes before me, I struggled to break free but was unable to break their grip. I went still and then, as a police constable I knew had once taught me, I kicked backwards as hard as I could; and when my foot connected with a captor's leg I dragged my right arm free. I swung round on my surprised captors, one of whom was now clutching his knee, and punched at the other. However, he caught my fist in his hand and having much greater strength than I, he easily restrained me. The other man sat on the floor of the chamber, cursing and swearing bitterly. The man still holding me slapped my face with his free hand. It felt like I'd been hit by an express train and I staggered. He let me fall to the floor and the one whose knee I had damaged kicked the side of my head as hard as he could with his other foot. Through the ringing in my ears I dimly heard Sheila scream again.

The Addanc's laughter ran across the chamber and stopped all the action. "Be still now," the monster called. With little apparent effort its voice was loud enough to hurt the ears and both of my captors obeyed and stopped what they were doing immediately. "Bring him here!" the Addanc commanded.

The two men took me by the arms again. The one whose knee was clearly hurting badly put his mouth close to my ear. "You're going to pay for that one," he hissed. "I'm going to work you over until you beg for the death the Master offers you." I had just enough self-respect left to ignore him. I was dragged up to the monster and thrown down roughly at its feet to sprawl on the floor beside Sheila.

"Hello, Mister Jones," she said with a wry smile.

"Sheila? Are you hurt?"

"Not yet."

"Sheila, There's…"

I was interrupted by a savage kick to the ribs that made me cry out and won me another, though less brutal, kick.

"Shut it, you. Now listen to the Master." One of my captors reinforced his command with a third kick that left me gasping for breath.

"Better and better." Now I paid attention to the monster before us. Looking up, I could see that the body and legs were those of a misshapen homunculus. There was no doubt it was male for it wore no clothing and was fully, loathsomely, erect. The erection dripped a thin stream of a luminous substance and I felt nauseous as I realised that it was the same liquid I had seen on the lips of the assembled followers of the Addanc. The head was that of a crocodile, with jet black eyes that held no pupils. Those eyes terrified me, for they were impersonal, dispassionate, cold, and held no hint or echo of humanity within them whatsoever. Again I felt absolutely and completely, terrified of this being..

"Make them drink," ordered the Addanc.

Rough hands seized my head and my jaws were pulled apart. I tried to bite the fingers but received instead a cuff around the head that made my eyes water and my consciousness reel. A bitter and vile liquid was forced into my mouth and a large hand was clamped over my nose and mouth until I had to swallow. The drink burned my mouth and throat, all the way down to my stomach, and I was allowed to drop to the floor. I lifted my arm and wiped my eyes clear with my sleeve in time to see Sheila treated the same way. The goblet dropped to the floor as the last of the liquid was poured down her throat.

"What the hell have you done to us?" I demanded through scalding lips. I heard Sheila whimper from the pain caused by swallowing the drink and again a rage ran through me. I pushed myself up from my knees and faced the monster. It was a little shorter than I, yet the age and power that radiated from it left me in no doubt that in every way imaginable it was my superior.

The Addanc tilted its head, considering first Sheila and then me. "Would you like to know what I have given you to drink?" it asked.

"Yes!" said Sheila fiercely.

The Addanc took a step back and looked around at the assembly. "Perhaps it will help you to know a little of my story," it said reflectively.

"Don't care!" replied Sheila. "What have you given me?"

She was ignored. "My people were the rulers of Prydain, the pre-eminent in the land and the most superior of the peoples who lived here. The other races acknowledged our lordship and oversaw every aspect of this ancient land." The Addanc paused reflectively. "But then we were overthrown by some who were jealous of us and our powers. My people were hunted and wherever we banded together to resist, we were assailed and killed." A tear ran slowly from one eye and I listened with surprise to the tale of years as the Addanc spoke of its people being driven at last to this one corner of the land. "And now, after all these years, I am the last of the Addanc. Solitary. Alone." It sighed, and beaten and abused as I had been, I could not help but feel sympathy for this creature, born to life but doomed to be alone - for how long? It spoke as if it had lived for centuries, back before our written history into the dreaming time of Old Britain. Had it been alone for all that time? I could not imagine how that must feel and when I cast a glance at Sheila I could see a tear falling from her eyes in sympathy for the creature that threatened us.

"But times change." The Addanc now sounded, brisk and businesslike. "I am tired of hiding from the ancient enemies of my people. Tired of living like a serf, dependent upon these meagre remnants of those who followed my people all those centuries ago. Time it is now for me to emerge, to rule as is my destiny as the last of my kind."

"But how?" asked Sheila. "You are but one, and these few

cannot do much. What do you think you are going to do when the police or the army find you?"

The Addanc threw back its head and laughed. "Let them come. Let them all come. Let them taste my vengeance, taste the real power of my people. As we declined and fell into mean ways, few of my race used our true powers and even argued that they had been our downfall. As if that could be possible! Now, last of a proud and noble people, I have no such scruple. You have tasted my power, although you do not yet appreciate it. Perhaps you will come to do so, if you live out the next few hours."

"Live the next hours? What do you mean?" I asked.

The Addanc bent down, its crocodile jaws close to my face. I tasted the cold breath and shuddered in revulsion. "That drink contained a taste of my people's oldest power. We can create and spread disease that kills such lesser beings as yourselves. We carry, and are immune to, many of the scourges that have from time to time wiped out thousands of your race. Who knows, maybe some of those epidemics were created by others like myself, living in isolation, fearful of you despite your puny bodies. When I again rule in Prydain, I will use the machines you yourselves have created to hunt for any remaining of my folk, and bring them here. Then together we shall bring a new age upon the world."

Sheila just looked at the Addanc, apparently shocked by what she had heard. I looked at the monster in horror. "Then you seek to poison half of the world, so that you can rule the rest?" I half whispered.

"Yes," replied the Addanc in satisfaction.

"These people here, what about them?" I asked loudly.

"They have no need to fear," replied their master. He gestured at his obscene loins. "I create enough of the antidote for them to be free of the fear of the disease I have chosen. They will be your rulers under my Overlordship. I merely have to allow them to take of it, as they and their families have done for generations beyond count."

"Assanc, Addanc, Addanc, Addanc, Assanc," moaned the assembly.

"Then..." I started, but my voice trailed into silence.

When I stopped speaking, the Addanc completed the sentence for me. "Yes. You have both been given doses of the disease I intend to spread. Rapid, virulent, the only cure is within me. You two will be held while the disease takes hold in you and then sent out into the world to spread my poison amongst the rest of your race."

"Doctors at the hospital will cure us!" I insisted.

"Ah, that is where those with a small pretension to medical knowledge pass their days. Hospitals. Yes, you should certainly go to a hospital; for once the infection spreads amongst the medical staff and takes hold, those with the only chance to halt my ascent to power will be gone. And I shall rule. Let your soldiers come, for they too we will infect with the disease: and when they have died, who will be bold enough to take their place and challenge me? Who could challenge me? None can challenge me!"

These last words were shouted, and the echoes ran around and around the underground chamber. I grabbed my stomach as a spasm of pain ran through it. I looked at Sheila; she was twisted upon the floor in agony. The Addanc laughed, the sound loud and frightening in that confined space, and then it leant towards me and asked me a question.

"Are you looking forward to your death, now?"

*

The broken wooden doors gave Eric enough cover to let him stand unseen almost within the chamber. He looked through the gap in the boards, and almost fell through the doors himself in shock as he watched Mister Jones appear in the chamber. Eric watched in horror as Mr Jones and Sheila were forced first to witness the obscene ritual, and then to drink from the goblet. He did not need to listen to the Addanc's words to understand that his friends had been forced to drink a poison that would fill them with disease. His sports bag lay near his feet, and Eric pulled back the zipper, opening the bag. The hilts of the silver swords he had himself crafted in his workshop at home lay on the top and he gripped one firmly with his right hand. After a moment's hesitation, he also drew the other sword with his left hand and returned to his vantage point.

The Addanc waved dismissively at his two captives. "Take them, and release them at some distance," it ordered. "Not too close to here, somewhere they will be found easily by those who have usurped my authority."

Mr Davis looked around the group. "Emlyn: you, Idris and Morgan should be enough. You can tie them up now, but that drink will have them asleep in twenty minutes. Then untie them and drop them at Yr Groes, the junction with the main road.

Ring the police from the payphone call box there and then get away."

Eric saw three of the men acknowledge the order. They each bowed low to the Addanc, and walked towards the two figures that lay prone on the floor before the monster. Eric's expression hardened and he gripped the hilts of the swords more firmly. Then he took a step back, and with his right foot kicked the sagging wooden doors as hard as he could at their join. The doors groaned and swung open: the left-hand door hit the wall and partly bounced back towards the passage, but the right-hand door fell from the ancient hinges and smashed onto the floor of the chamber. Splinters flew as the door came apart and lay in ruin.

"I so like to make an entrance," Eric remarked into the sudden silence as he stepped into the chamber.

The Addanc stared at the intruder. Led by Iuan Davis, his followers moved as one towards Eric but the Addanc bid them stop.

Eric waved at Sheila and Mister Jones, using one of the silver swords to emphasise his point. "Let them go."

The Addanc gave Eric a long, searching, considered, examination. "I think I knew you, once," it said slowly. "Long, long ago."

Eric nodded abruptly. "And I knew you. Now, let them go."

The Addanc shrugged. "They can go." Mr Davis scowled, but his master ignored him.

"They have drunk of the Waters of Lethe, you know," it told

Eric.

"I know," Eric replied. "What of it?"

"I was not proposing to give them the antidote. They can go with you and carry the contagion with them. After all, that is all that I desire."

"Your desire I know. It is meaningless, and will not prevail."

Eric transferred his attention to Sheila and Mister Jones. "Come over here, you two." In his peripheral vision he saw movement, and one of the silver swords swept upwards. Emlyn stopped in his tracks. The chamber was lit by a red light and in that glare the silver swords took on a sheen as if they shone with wet blood. That threat halted Emlyn as surely as a direct command from his Master, the Addanc. Mister Jones managed to get to his knees and helped Sheila to sit up. He looked at the Addanc as the creature loomed above him.

"You may go," confirmed the Addanc, smiling.

Sheila shook her head and vomited a foul looking liquid over the Addanc's feet. The monster seemed unconcerned.

"Worthless gesture," it told her. The Addanc's voice was bitter, cold and amused at the same time. "The disease has entered your system now. You may flee with your friends, but there is no cure that you will find outside of this chamber."

Involuntarily Sheila's glance slipped down the Addanc's deformed body to the source of the antidote to the poison: "I'd rather die," she said briefly.

"I'm sure that wish will be granted," replied the Addanc. "As it will be to many of your race when you leave here, starting with - him - over there."

Mister Jones managed to get up with an effort. He clutched his side with one hand and breathed heavily. Sheila took his arm and pulled him away from the Addanc.

"So, you reject me a third time," said the creature. "Three times is the charm. There will be no return for you."

Sheila ignored the Addanc and pulled again at Mister Jones' arm. They walked unsteadily towards Eric, who waited for them with a set expression.

"If you can, make him vomit," Eric instructed Sheila as she went past him. She nodded.

"Eric, how... why...?"

"This is not the time or place, Sheila." Eric did not take his eyes away from the Addanc as he spoke. Sheila pulled Mister Jones past Eric to the entrance to the passageway back to Clyffe House. Mister Jones sank to his knees, and forced one finger into his mouth.

"What are you doing?" hissed Sheila.

"Sick. Make myself sick. As Eric said." Mister Jones replied, and gagged. Sheila stepped to one side, as Mister Jones vomited. He promptly forced a finger down his throat again.

Eric ignored the sounds behind him, and kept his gaze on the Addanc. It moved uneasily.

"You seem very familiar to me," the Addanc said. It started to walk towards Eric, but Eric swept one of the silver swords in a gleaming arc and the Addanc stopped. "Do not think that those can hurt me," it remarked in a conversational tone. "There are those to whom that metal is anathema; but I am not of that order of beings."

"Maybe. But they are sharp enough to kill," replied Eric. He glanced to his left, raised the sword in that hand and pointed it directly at Iuan Davis who had been trying to move closer to Eric while his attention was on the Addanc. "Especially you," Eric said to Mr Davis.

The Addanc shrugged. "None have challenged me for centuries."

"That," Eric cut in quickly, "is because you and your evil dreams have been in hiding here, away from the world that rejected you centuries ago. This world has moved on and you have no place in it now."

"No place?" shouted the Addanc. Several people put their hands over their ears. "*No place?* Before my kin were driven from this land in ruin we ruled here. This IS our place, Prydain IS our land, MY land. And I mean to take it back!"

"The Prydain you knew died centuries ago. Now it is the time of men, not legends."

"Men," sneered the Addanc. "I know men. They cower, they bow, and they serve. They are slaves to me."

Several of the assembled men around the pool looked less than pleased at this statement, but the Addanc ignored them and continued. "Yes, some of them are loyal to me, but they are loyal because the power I grant to them binds them to me."

Behind Eric, Mister Jones was sick for a second time.

"That will not remove my power from his body," said the Addanc, relaxing somewhat and staring dispassionately at Mister Jones. "The sickness is within him now and when you take him from this place he will die; and in dying he will spread the contagion I desire amongst his people."

"Really?" asked Mister Jones, standing upright with some difficulty. Sheila supported him by the arm, although she too looked unwell.

"Yes," said the Addanc, disdainfully. "But take heart; your death matters to me, for it is a step towards my rightful heritage."

Mister Jones pushed himself away from the wall of the chamber and moved to stand beside Eric. His left hand still clutched his ribs; but with his right hand he took one of the silver swords from Eric's left hand. Eric resisted a little at first, then gave way. Mister Jones raised the sword and pointed it at the Addanc.

"If you assail me with that, you will die," the Addanc told him.

"But I'm going to die anyway, or so you just told me," Mister Jones replied.

The Addanc hesitated. Then Iuan Davis walked towards Mister Jones. "You'd best give that to me, Mister Jones," said Mr Davis.

"Not a chance."

Mr Davis moved closer, and only stopped when Mister Jones swung the point of the sword close to his chest. The red sheen on the blade was briefly reflected across his throat, and Mr Davis swallowed.

"Hit him with it, Mister Jones," called Sheila from the passageway.

"Take it from him," instructed the Addanc.

Mr Davis raised his hand and Mister Jones twisted the sword tip towards his face, before wincing at the pain in his side. His blade drooped. Mr Davis grabbed for the hand that was holding the sword but jumped back with a screech of pain when Eric ran his sword through the upper part of Mr Davis' arm. Eric's sword now ran with a trickle of blood and the Addanc licked its lips.

"This has gone far enough," Eric said firmly.

"Not yet. You still live," replied the Addanc, casting a hungry eye on the blood running down the blade of Eric's sword.

"My arm! I can't use my arm, Lord!" shouted Iuan Davis.

"Fear not, it doesn't matter," replied the Addanc, absently.

"What do you mean, it doesn't matter?" demanded Mr Davis, turning to face the Addanc.

"What your master means is this," said Eric, "he has killed you with his poison and you will carry the infection to your families who will die also."

Some of the followers of the Addanc shifted uneasily, and muttered.

"Nonsense," said the Addanc. "Who is this man? What do you think he knows of me and my power?"

Eric opened the neck of his shirt with his left hand, and shook loose a medallion upon a silver chain. The Addanc gasped, and took a step backwards.

"Where did you get *that*?" the Addanc demanded.

Eric smiled. "I think you know. And you know this ring, too." He held up his left hand, and the red light of the chamber was reflected from a jewel set upon a ring Eric wore on the middle finger. "Do you remember?"

The Addanc stepped back again and staggered as it bumped into the ornate chair.

"What of this poison, Master?" shouted one of the assembly.

"You have the antidote. It will not harm you, as it has not harmed you in the years you have taken it already."

"But this time it isn't the same, is it?" asked Eric, raising his voice so that all the group could hear him. "This time you mean these men to carry the disease out into their world, to infect their families, their friends, their children and their neighbours, to spread your poison wide; that is what you mean, is it not?" He took a step towards the Addanc and the monster backed away again.

"Listen not!" ordered the Addanc. "Listen not, and believe in me as you have done all these years!"

Mister Jones heaved, and was sick again. Mr Davis moved away from him, still holding his arm. Blood oozed between his fingers. Eric made a fist with his left hand and raised it above his shoulder.

The Addanc howled. "Do not!" it commanded. "Do not," it repeated, but the second time its tone was less peremptory and more appealing; "you cannot know what that ring can call."

"What makes you think I do not know?" asked Eric. "What makes you think I have not used it before?"

"Because you live! None now living could use that ring." The Addanc looked around at its followers, who stared back in a sullen silence. "That ring summons one who will slay all you mortals in this chamber. Do not let him call..."

"Call who?" asked Mr Davis.

"Call what?" muttered Alwyn from his place in the circle behind the Addanc. Those beside him shifted uneasily.

"Rakasha!" cried the Addanc. "That ring can summon demons from your worst dreams, and they will rend and slay you all!"

There was a murmur of anger from the men, but also the murmur held an unmistakeable edge of fear and Eric heard that. "They will do what they should have done centuries ago, and end your evil," Eric said loudly to the Addanc. He turned briefly to Mister Jones and said softly: "You and Sheila get behind me and stand very close with a hand each on my shoulder. Whatever you do, do not let go of me or each other."

Mister Jones moved behind Eric and beckoned urgently to Sheila. She walked nervously away from the passageway and stood beside him. He started whispering in her ear.

"What's a Rakasha?" asked Emlyn, loudly.

"An evil demon!" cried the Addanc. "Quickly, upon him and seize that ring before he summons the creature here amongst us, with its desire to eat human flesh!"

"Not this human flesh," retorted Eric. He looked around at the men who stood beside the pool, their faces variously marked with greater or lesser sores and calluses and pockmarks; the signs of the disease they carried. "Because you have poisoned them, haven't you? And that antidote you claim they have received, that is no real antidote is it? It is the start of a process to turn them into beings like yourself!"

The Addanc stepped backwards again: "You know? How do you know?" It dropped its head for a moment. The followers of the Addanc stirred and then were still, staring at their master. Some showed horror and fear on their faces, others delight and excitement. "Have you any idea what it has been like for me down these centuries?" The Addanc's voice was little more than a whisper, and all present had to strain to hear the words. "I have been alone, the last of my kind. I live, I live and I need the fellowship of my own kind. My kin."

"So down the years you have sought to change the men who live here into images of yourself?" Eric somehow managed to blend both disgust and pity into his voice. The chamber was very still.

"Yes. But it has not been easy. The genetic makeup of these humans is strong, and it has been hard; it has taken me many lives of men to bring these here to a point where they may change to become my new kind. My new kin."

"You mean we are to change into you, Lord?" asked Iuan Davis.

Several of the group felt their faces and bodies, as if they could feel themselves starting to distort. Some looked excited, others horrified, all fearful.

"I doubt it," insisted Eric. "I believe this creature has tried before. And failed. It is more likely that you will die, and in dying kill your families, friends and many who live around here."

"You said our families would be protected!" shouted Alwyn.

"They will be," replied the Addanc.

"I don't believe you," replied Alwyn. "I think you are lying!"

"I am your god!" shouted the Addanc.

"Making us in your image are you?" asked another of those standing around the pool. "I don't want this anymore."

"You will obey me!"

"I think I've been caught in a bad dream," Alwyn said. "And I'm just awakening." He looked at Eric. "Can you save us?"

"I don't know," replied Eric.

Behind him, Mister Jones stirred uneasily. His face was very pale.

"But I can stop him from hurting more people," Eric continued, pointing at the Addanc with his sword. "How many of your forefathers died unpleasantly, poisoned by this being's attempts to create a new race to serve him?" he asked. "You!" he addressed the Addanc again. "You are not divine and you do not own the power to create, only to twist, spoil, unmake and destroy! That is why your kind were returned to the Void all those years ago. How you escaped, I do not know. And I feel saddened by your pain and loss down these long years, and that must end."

With a determined expression, Eric raised his left hand high into the air and cried aloud.

"How do you know those words?" screamed the Addanc. "How?"

Eric did not reply, but lowered his hand until the glowing ring pointed directly at the Addanc. The water in the pool began to swirl and heave, then boiled upwards in a wild manner akin to a geyser before falling back to the surface with a mighty splash, then rising again into a tall pillar. The pillar shed drips and drops, then shuddered, and on the surface of the pool there now stood a nightmare being made from water. It threw back its head and howled, and the sound rang and echoed around the underground chamber. Several men fell to their knees, Mister Jones amongst them. Sheila crouched down to help him. Water began to lap over the side of the pool, and several men backed away from the poolside. The water checked when it reached the painted circle around the edge of the pool, then flowed over it. Sparks flashed as it passed, then died. The red light in the chamber began to fail.

"Rakasha!" screamed the Addanc, showing its fear.

"One hand on him, one hand on me!" Eric told Sheila. "Then shut your eyes!" Using his sword, Eric traced a circle on the floor around the three of them, as the Rakasha grew in size until it touched the roof of the chamber.

The Addanc screamed again and turned. It started to run towards the altar, and then changed its mind and headed for the passage down which Mister Jones had come, the passage to the outside of the hill. Soundlessly at first, then with an explosion of noise the waters burst from the pool and flooded the chamber in moments. The torrent rushed around the walls creating currents and eddies, throwing the Addanc helplessly back towards the Rakasha that waited patiently in the centre of the chamber. Inside the circle drawn by Eric, all was still and dry; outside it the waters raged. The Addanc's followers were tossed and spun helplessly in the tumult. Then with an awful suction the waters were withdrawn, leaving only Eric and his two companions and the Water Demon of the Rakasha. The Addanc, the men who had followed it, the ornate Throne, the altar - all were gone.

Eric raised the glowing ring to the Water Demon and spoke its dismissal; the Rakasha bowed, and sank back into the pool and was gone. Beside the pool stood a silver flask, worked about with ancient images gods, demons and men. Eric bowed, then dropped to his knees, panting.

"Eric?" asked Sheila. "What was that... that... that...?"

"That, Sheila was a Water Rakasha, a being of energy that prefers to take its form from water, when enough is available." Eric's face was grey with fatigue.

"How did it come here then?"

"I called it. I have a ring that gives the wearer dominion over such beings - for as long as their strength holds out."

"And then?"

Eric gave her a faint smile. "It is traditional for demons to turn on those who call them if their strength fades, or is insufficient."

Sheila looked around the chamber. The rushing waters had scoured it clean of everything, and only a faint glow of light from the passageway to the outside let her see.

"The Addanc... those people who worshipped it, where have they gone?"

"Best not to ask."

"Why?" demanded Sheila.

"Well, the fact I don't really know is one reason. That I don't think we would like to know is another."

"And the Addanc?" Sheila hesitated. "I felt sorry for him - for it - there. To be alone for all those years because your friends and family have been killed. That's dreadful."

"I know," said Eric. He looked away so that Sheila could not see his face. "But that does not excuse his evil, or his plan to kill so many people, does it?" Behind him, Mister Jones heaved and was sick again. Eric flinched and turned to look at his friends. Sheila was very pale, and Mister Jones was clearly in some distress. "Sheila, do you see that flask over there near the pool?"

"Yes, Eric."

"Go and get it. Drink some, and then make Mister Jones drink all the rest. Better hurry. Oh, and I want that goblet."

Mister Jones slipped sideways, and lay on the floor, twitching.

"Hurry!"

Sheila approached the silver flask carefully and stretched out her hand as if scared the flask would bite her or greet her with an electric shock. She was surprised when neither of those things happened. She picked up the goblet, but dropped that as she knelt down beside Mister Jones.

"Drink!" ordered Eric. He dropped his silver sword and knelt down with Sheila beside Mister Jones. "Sheila! He's going!" he hissed. Mister Jones' breathing became ragged and began to slow as the Addanc's poisoned drink began to take its final hold on him. "Sheila!"

Sheila nervously pulled the stopper from the top of the flask and took a drink. She had expected the fluid to be dreadful, but instead it tasted faintly of peaches. She swallowed, and pushed the stopper back into the flask.

"Hurry!" cried Eric. He rolled Mister Jones onto his back, and raised his head. "The flask, or it will be too late!"

Sheila turned and frantically hurried back across the wet and slippery floor. She thrust the flask at Eric who grabbed it from her. Her pulled the stopper out with his teeth and poured the liquid into Mister Jones' mouth. Mister Jones coughed and some of the peach flavoured fluid ran from his mouth. Eric tipped the flask again.

"Swallow!" he ordered, and tilted Mister Jones' head backwards. By reflex action alone, Mister Jones swallowed. He coughed again, but his breathing strengthened. Eric tilted the flask again, and this time Mister Jones drank eagerly. He sighed deeply and relaxed in Eric's arms.

"Is he... dead?" asked Sheila.

"Don't think so," replied Eric.

"Dying?"

"We are all dying, Sheila. Day by day. But he isn't going to die today. Nor are you, thanks to that remedy."

"What's in it?" Sheila knelt down beside Eric, and looked at her neighbour and friend.

"I don't know. But I do know it will be a remedy for whatever that filth was the Addanc made you drink. As long as we got enough inside him in time."

"It wasn't bad, but I think I'd have preferred some merlot." Mister Jones' voice was hoarse and ragged.

"Mister Jones!" Sheila flung her arms around him, and Mister Jones shook his head wearily.

"I take it you won?" he asked Eric.

"I think so, Mister Jones."

"Then if you don't mind helping me a little, I think I'd quite like to get out of here. I suppose that this chamber is about to collapse in on us?"

Eric laughed. "No. It seems quite secure."

"But it's a bit damp. Unhealthy, I'd say. That tunnel I used to come in here will get us outside quickly." Mister Jones was understandably keen to get out of the cave as quickly as possible.

Eric, with some difficulty, pulled Mister Jones to his feet. Sheila put her shoulder under Mister Jones' other arm. Eric pushed the goblet into his sports bag and picked it up. He looked around the chamber. "Let's go," he said briefly. They headed for the passage leading to the outside. A cold wind blew in from the hillside beyond and Mister Jones lifted his head and filled his lungs with clean air.

"It's over," he said.

Eric looked at the end of the goblet, not fully within his bag, and considered his reply. "For now, perhaps," he agreed, looking at the faded remains of a label. "For now."

Epilogue

Silence reigned over Clyffe House. Silence dripped from the darkly varnished roof beams that looked so quaint in the daylight. Silence stole through the single glazed windows, and filtered down the chimney in the living room as the last embers of the fire flickered bravely and died. Silence rose from the sink in the kitchen, and dripped from the taps in the bathroom, flooding out under the closed doors into the corridor and sliding inexorably down past the front door towards the occupied bedrooms, cresting like a small wave before flowing below the varnished doors and filling the rooms beyond, rising to the meet the dripping roof beams.

Silent too were the feet that made the wet footprints that led from the kitchen door to the far end of the hall, and stopped at the door leading to the end room. The Addanc was gone, but its death had not freed those who did not quite live in Clyffe House. They waited for their next visitor.

Alone in his home, Eric held the goblet retrieved from the Addanc's cavern in his hands. He turned it over and over, looking at the carvings with some distaste. However he continually upended the goblet and looked at it. On the bottom was a small sticker showing a catalogue number. This was a mystery to be solved. What sort of warehouse would carry such an item, and more worryingly - what else might it hold? With a sense of unfinished business, Eric put the goblet into a velvet bag, and stowed it away in a cupboard.

ABOUT THE AUTHOR

Will Macmillan Jones lives in Wales, a lovely green, verdant land with a rich cultural heritage. He does his best to support this heritage by drinking the local beer and shouting loud encouragement whenever International Rugby is on the TV. A fifty something lover of blues, rock and jazz he has just fulfilled a lifetime ambition by filling an entire wall of his home office with (full) bookcases. When not writing, he is usually lost with the help of a SatNav on top of a large hill in the middle of nowhere, looking for dragons. He hasn't found one yet, but insists that it is only a matter of time.

His major comic fantasy series, released by Red Kite Publishing, can be found at:

www.thebannedunderground.com

and information on his other work and stuff in general at :

www.willmacmillanjones.com

Printed in Great Britain
by Amazon

27271744R00118